"How dare you abduct me, Captain Hawkins."

A black brow arched. "This is not an abduction, my lady — this is an arrest."

Her throat closed even tighter. Was he frightening her? Or would he truly hand her over to the authorities? He wouldn't dare, she thought. The scandal!

Softening her posture, she said in her most feminine voice, "Cousin William."

"Cousin Madeline," he mimicked in a merciless tone.

He would not be moved by any supplications of family ties, the brute, and she finally sighed in defeat. "Cousin Maddie will do," she offered. "I trust we can come to a discreet arrangement?"

"An arrangement?"

"There's no need to create a public stir, ruining my dear cousin's wedding night."

His growl skittered over her spine.

"No need, indeed. Very well, Cousin Maddie, you will take me to your home and hand over the stolen jewels — and I won't escort you to the gallows."

Madeline swallowed a heavy lump in her throat.

"The jewels or the gallows, my lady?"

ROMANCES BY **Alexandra Benedict**

The Hawkins Brothers Series
Mistress of Paradise
The Infamous Rogue
The Notorious Scoundrel
How to Seduce a Pirate
How to Steal a Pirate's Heart
All I Want for Christmas is a Pirate

The Too/Westmore Brothers Series
Too Great a Temptation
Too Scandalous to Wed
Too Dangerous to Desire

The Fallen Ladies Society
The Princess and the Pauper

Stand Alone Romance
A Forbidden Love

Anthology
Tales of Forbidden Love

Young Adult Fiction
So Down I Fall

ALEXANDRA BENEDICT

How to Steal a Pirate's Heart

This book is a work of fiction. Names, characters, places, and incidents are products of the author's imagination and are used fictitiously. Any resemblance to actual events, locales, or persons, living or dead, is entirely coincidental.

www.AlexandraBenedict.ca

To Olivia.

Welcome to the family!

The Hawkins Family Tree

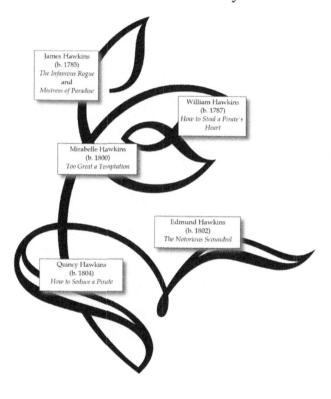

James Hawkins
(b. 1785)
The Infamous Rogue
and
Mistress of Paradise

William Hawkins
(b. 1787)
How to Steal a Pirate's Heart

Mirabelle Hawkins
(b. 1800)
Too Great a Temptation

Edmund Hawkins
(b. 1802)
The Notorious Scoundrel

Quincy Hawkins
(b. 1804)
How to Seduce a Pirate

How to Steal a Pirate's Heart

CHAPTER 1

London, 1827

Captain William Hawkins stood on the terrace outside his sister's fashionable townhouse in the heart of Mayfair. The noise and frippery inside the ballroom had triggered another throbbing headache, and he'd escaped the celebration in search of peace. The secluded garden, awash in milky moonlight, offered him tranquility, and he observed the gaiety through the glass terrace doors without feeling the disagreeable effects.

"There you are, Will."

His youngest brother Quincy stepped onto the terrace, two crystal tumblers in hand.

The pup handed him a drink. "It's a brilliant affair, isn't it, Will? A celebration to remember for a hundred years. Amy looks prettier than a princess. And Eddie can't stop grinning. Can you believe it? Eddie!" He sighed. "They're finally going to be happy. It's about bloody time."

William watched the twirling newlyweds, both resplendent in their fancy duds. He shared Quincy's sentiment. His otherwise surly middle brother, Edmund, and his dashing bride, Lady Amy, had suffered enough hardship to last a lifetime.

"About time, indeed," said William. The twinge in his head worsened, and he clenched his eyes, grimacing.

"Are you all right?"

"Fine," he clipped. "It's just a headache."

"Tough luck, old fellow."

William snorted at the "old fellow" bit. At forty, he was seventeen years Quincy's senior, and ever since he'd reached the pinnacle age, his tactless brother had found it particularly amusing.

As music swelled into the night, Quincy remarked, "Belle really knows how to host a smashing reception."

After rubbing the bridge of his nose, William turned his gaze toward his sister, Mirabelle, the Duchess of Wembury. She was dancing with her husband, her cheeks flushed, so full of life. Two short years ago, she had almost died giving birth to her son. Even now William's chest tightened at the agonizing memory.

As they had all learned at one time or another life was precious, and momentous occasions needed to be marked with the proper fanfare—meaning food, drink and merrymaking galore.

A gust of laughter filled the terrace through the half open doors.

"Blimey," from Quincy. "Now that's a sound you don't hear every day."

William recognized the unusual merriment as belonging to his eldest brother, Captain James Hawkins, the once infamous pirate Black Hawk. The man had the temperament of a raging bull, and his sudden, spirited outburst could only be attributed to one source.

Sure enough, William located James with his exotic wife Sophia, ensconced in a tête-à-tête near the ballroom doors. Whatever their exchange, it had amused the former corsair to no end.

The Hawkins brothers were happy. At last. After years at sea as notorious pirates, they had settled into the roles of gentlemen, relations to a distinguished duchess. Even Quincy had much improved, a crippling melancholy having consumed him for years. But the pup had also recently wed, his wife's healing touch having chased away his nightmares.

"A toast," said Quincy, raising his glass. "To happily-ever-after. Though late, 'tis better than never."

William offered a sardonic smile. Unlike the rest of his hard-drinking brothers, he never wallowed in alcohol. He didn't like to lose control of his senses. Ever. But more and more of late he'd made exceptions.

He clinked his brother's glass before downing the fiery brandy. Why not? thought William. After all, he was dying.

At the sharp pain in his skull, William winced and dropped the tumbler, the crystal shattering, vertigo pushing him toward the ground.

Quincy grabbed his arm and steadied him. "Whoa, old fellow. The headache again? Or you can't hold your drink?"

The pup's smirk faded when William didn't—couldn't—answer. Quincy quickly took his brother's arm and wrapped it around his sturdy shoulder, supporting him. "I'll fetch help."

"No," he gritted. "It's *their* night. I won't dampen it with a bleedin' headache."

"All right then."

The pup swiveled him around the terrace and steered him toward a secluded bench.

William collapsed on the seat, groaning, his pulsing brow in his hands.

"A cold compress?" suggested Quincy.

"No," he returned. "It won't help."

Nothing would help.

For several months, William had suffered inexplicable headaches. And then the bleeding had started. From his nose. His gums.

Just like father.

Their father, Drake Hawkins, had died seven years ago from the same mysterious illness. The symptoms had been identical: headaches and spontaneous bleedings. Soon William would lose stamina. Then breath. Then life.

If he measured his father's demise against his own, William wagered he'd six months remaining, eight at the most. He had yet to tell any of his siblings. He just hadn't the words.

"There's catmint in the herbal garden," said Quincy. "I'll have a servant boil the leaves, make a tea. It'll dull the headache."

"Aye," he drawled. "Thanks."

Quincy left the terrace.

A tea wouldn't cure his ails, but it wasn't the right time to reveal the truth, though he would have to soon. He couldn't maintain the pretense of robust health much longer.

He'd already put his affairs in order. As a privateer in the Royal Navy's African Squadron, he'd resigned his post with the Admiralty. There would be no more sea patrols off the coast of West Africa, hunting illegal British slavers. If a headache paralyzed him in the heat of battle, he'd risk losing his ship, his entire crew.

He had completed his last will and testament, bequeathing his ship to his oldest brother and assigning generous pensions to his crew. His bachelor residence would go to his two youngest siblings. And he'd set aside a series of personal items for his sister, the duchess. He hoped she'd keep his memory alive, telling swashbuckling tales to his niece and nephew of their Uncle William. There was just one thing left to do — tell his family he was dying.

In a few minutes, Quincy returned with the steaming tea. "Drink." He handed him the herbal brew, his expression troubled. "What's the matter, Will?"

"A headache, I told you." And he poured the piping balm down his gullet for good measure. "I'll be fine."

The headache would pass, as always, and he'd return to full strength — until the next assault.

William wiped his mouth and placed the porcelain cup on the bench. "I just need rest. Go back to the ball, Quincy. Enjoy yourself."

The pup observed him for several critical moments before he shrugged. "All right, but I'll return to check on you . . . Will, your nose."

William reached for his face. When he pulled his hand away, a splotch of blood was smeared across his fingers. "Shit."

His brother handed him a kerchief. "What's the matter with you?"

"Damn it." He snatched the linen and pressed it under his nose. "I don't need you to play nursemaid. Leave!"

But Quincy retreated as far back as the shrubs, then crossed his arms over his chest, not budging a step more. "Tell me," he demanded.

"I don't take orders from you, pup."

"I can help—"

"No," he snapped. "You can't help."

Since boyhood, Quincy had possessed a healing touch. He even served aboard William's ship as surgeon. But he couldn't cure this malady. No one could. William had consulted prestigious physicians in London, medicine men in Africa. But there was no treatment.

No hope.

"You're sick, Will."

"The devil I am."

A silence then settled between them. A seemingly interminable silence. And William knew his brother had just discovered his secret, that he'd recognized William's symptoms.

Slowly William lifted his head. "Not. One. Word."

The silence stretched.

"Did you hear me, pup?" He growled, "Not *one* word."

"I have to tell the others."

William wasn't a violent man, he wasn't even bad

tempered, but he had an unmistakable urge to thrash his sibling if the young man refused to keep silent.

As his head pounded ever harder, he gnashed his teeth. "*I* will tell the others when *I'm* good and ready, so don't breathe a bloody word—to anyone."

After another round of agonizing quiet, Quincy finally bobbed his head. He stared at William a second more, his expression inscrutable, before he quit the terrace and sauntered back inside the ballroom.

William watched his most talkative kin through the glass doors. He sighed after a short time, relieved the pup hadn't approached any of their siblings. Instead, Quincy had settled to one side of the ballroom, alone, his features impassive.

His brow pulsing with explosive pressure, William kneaded his temples. The stone-cold look of shock on his brother's face didn't augur easy times ahead.

William imagined the flare of emotions that would erupt from the rest of his tempestuous family when he at last revealed his illness. If they greeted the news with similar silence or more characteristic shouting, the end result would still be deafening. And his headache worsened at the grueling thought.

How was he going to tell them? *When* was he going to tell them? Soon it would be impossible to hide his symptoms, yet he dreaded making the admission.

Almost an hour later, William's headache finally abated. His strength gradually returned, and he regained his footing, moving off the bench.

As he sauntered back toward the terrace, the

unmistakable sound of rattling wheels captured his notice. He peered over the hedge groves and spotted an unmarked carriage rounding the street corner, travelling at great speed.

His innards tightened.

Trouble.

William dashed through the garden toward the front gate just as the vehicle rolled to a stop at the entrance. He fisted his palms before he wrenched open the door — and stilled.

Light from the overhead gas lamp pooled around a billowing gold skirt with taffeta underpinnings and an embroidered hemline. Soon a feminine face emerged from the darkness and leaned toward him, smiling.

"Goodness, what a reaming reception. But you've every right to chastise me. I'm terribly late."

His muscles stiffened at the provocative thought before he shoved aside the uncharacteristic impulse. Her deep green eyes complimented her ringed, ginger brown hair, heaped upon her head and fastened with a pearl comb. She appeared in her thirtieth year. Dark brows and full rose lips added color to her fair complexion, while high cheeks bones and a fine nose balanced her sensual features.

"Did Lady Amy send you to wait for me? She must be very anxious, indeed." The woman offered her gloved hand. "Take me to her, if you please. I must apologize for my delay."

But William wasn't so easily bewitched by a pretty face. His instincts still screamed trouble.

Even as the woman's warm gaze burrowed into him, he pushed aside her spell-casting charm and stuck his head inside the vehicle.

She gasped at his uninvited proximity, her heated breath caressing his ear, her lavender perfume teasing his senses. The titillation disarmed him for a moment before he focused on the interior once more, searching the squabs.

Assured there was no threat — at least not to the bride and groom — William stepped away from the vehicle.

A set of piercing green eyes shot daggers at him.

"I beg your pardon." He bowed, then offered his hand. "Captain William Hawkins, brother of the groom, at your service."

After a moment of dubious reflection, the woman accepted his hand and descended the carriage. "Lady Madeline Winters, cousin to the bride."

"Forgive me, my lady. I have a duty to protect my brother and sister-in-law."

"From *moi*?"

"From Lady Amy's former husband, the Marquis of Gravenhurst."

A year ago, Lady Amy had been forced to wed the Marquis of Gravenhurst, a brutal fiend intent upon her family's destruction. The villain would have murdered Amy on their wedding night if Edmund hadn't saved her life, but before the marquis could be apprehended, the devil had escaped, his whereabouts still a mystery. And while Lady Amy had recently obtained an annulment, the danger remained that the marquis might return to complete his revenge.

"Of course, I understand," she murmured and opened her lace fan, fluttering the air, stirring the fine hairs at her temples. "If you will excuse me, Captain Hawkins, I must greet the newlyweds and atone for my unfashionable tardiness."

Sweeping up one side of her shimmering skirt, she sashayed through the gate then entranceway with the confidence of a royal princess, disappearing inside the glowing ballroom.

Still feeling strangely uneasy, William wandered back into the garden. Through the glass terrace doors, he observed his family as they warmly welcomed Lady Madeline with festive embraces. Something cold pierced his heart at the sight. It spread like ice through his veins.

"You have no soul, Will. You can't bleed. You don't even know love."

His eldest brother had accused him of heartless indifference not too long ago. And while the charge had only annoyed him then, it now gnawed at him without surcease, for as the end rolled near, William wondered if all the self-restraint and responsibility and stoicism had really done him any good. Had he missed an important aspect of life because he'd tried so damn hard to restrain his passionate Hawkins blood?

The unnerving thought festered in his soul. He suddenly found it difficult to breathe. About to turn away from all the familial gaiety, a flash of movement snagged his attention.

William sharpened his astute gaze on Lady Madeline. The woman offered a throaty laugh as she funned with an unsuspecting miss . . . then stealthy unclasped the chit's diamond bracelet and slipped it into her reticule.

CHAPTER 2

Madeline ducked behind the potted ferns, her heart pounding. She took several breaths before her pulse steadied and she regained her poise.

She would never grow accustomed to such audacious risks, but grave matters called for grave measures. With another valuable tucked inside her reticule, she had nearly reached her goal. Just a few more carefully selected pieces from a few more frivolous misses' and she'd have the funds she so desperately needed.

After smoothing her skirt and tweaking her satin gloves, Madeline gathered another hardy breath and stepped away from the secluded shrubbery—when an uncouth hand clinched her arm and dragged her back behind the feathered ferns.

"Unhand me!"

Her protest was cut short by a pair of piercing blue eyes penetrating straight to her soul. As her grandfather would've exclaimed: *shiver my top-sails.*

Captain William Hawkins glared at her with all the gentlemanly finesse of a cutthroat, and Madeline's heart surged again. The craggy fingers of doom gripped her throat, shrinking her airway, as she realized she'd made a dreadful mistake plundering at the ball.

From the moment she'd capped eyes on the captain, she'd sensed his cold indifference, his savvy insight. He wouldn't allow a fleck of dust to pass under his nose unobserved, she'd suspected. And yet the temptation of so many jewels had weakened her judgment. Blast it!

In her most placating voice, Madeline cooed, "Captain Hawkins—"

Air whooshed from her lungs as she staggered. The captain maneuvered her through the terrace doors and into the garden with fluid strides. Another polished swivel and jig, and a dizzy Madeline found herself stuffed inside a dark carriage with one nettled man.

The vehicle lurched. She teetered. A strong hand reached for her. It failed to secure her, though. Instead, it snatched the reticule from her wrist— allowing her to ignominiously topple over the squab.

Recovering her balance, Madeline sniffed with indignation. "How dare you abduct me, Captain Hawkins."

A black brow arched. "This is not an abduction, my lady—this is an arrest."

Her throat closed even tighter. Was he frightening her? Or would he truly hand her over to the authorities? He wouldn't dare, she thought. The scandal! And they were family . . . Yes, they were family. In-laws of some sort. Surely, he wouldn't toss his kin into the gaol?

Softening her posture, she said in her most

feminine voice, "Cousin William."

"Cousin Madeline," he mimicked in a merciless tone.

He would not be moved by any supplications of family ties, the brute, and she finally sighed in defeat. "Cousin Maddie will do," she offered. "I trust we can come to a discreet arrangement?"

"An arrangement?"

"There's no need to create a public stir, ruining my dear cousin's wedding night."

His growl skittered over her spine.

"No need, indeed. Very well, Cousin Maddie, you will take me to your home and hand over the other stolen jewels—and I won't escort you to the gallows."

The tension in the carriage thickened like smoke. She reached for the window, pinching it open. "I have no other stolen jewels."

"Liar," he charged. "You are the Light Finger Jewel Thief. I've read about you in the broadsheets. For several months, you've pilfered valuables from aristocrats across Town."

"I-I only pinched the bracelet tonight, I swear." Her blood roared in her ears as her heart thudded with the ferocity of a caged beast. "I have *no* other jewels."

"Your sleight of hand condemns you, I'm afraid. I've been at sea for twenty-five years. And in that time, I've met a pirate or two." He leaned forward, his eyes black as onyx. "And you are a pirate, Cousin Maddie."

"Rubbish."

"Enough! Edmund is a Bow Street Runner. How

would it appear if his cousin-in-law, a notorious thief, pillaged the city and he did nothing to prevent it? There would be an outcry. A demand for his head. Corruption, the crowd would chant. Lawlessness. And perhaps Lady Amy would become a widowed bride."

Madeline swallowed a heavy lump in her throat.

"The jewels or the gallows, my lady?"

His facetious "my lady" strangled her airway even more. He cared not a jot about what happened to her, only his brother and sister-in-law. Hope flittered from her heart. She was doomed. And so was her grandfather.

No! cried a defiant voice in her head. She had not come so far, waded through such perilous circumstances to surrender her *only* chance at ransoming her grandfather. If Captain Hawkins would not negotiate like a gentleman, then she would act like the pirate he accused her of being— she would give no quarters.

Madeline clamped her hands together in feigned resignation. "Very well, Captain Hawkins." And she confessed her address.

He shouted directions to the driver before settling back against the squab, and they spent the remainder of the journey in taut silence.

~ * ~

"This is your home?"

As William entered the library, Madeline wondered if he was incredulous or indifferent or mocking in his tone. She had never met a man with such powerful reservation. He was impossible to read. And that worried her a might.

"Cozy, isn't it?" she quipped.

He passed the cases of ancient maps and marine specimens and tribal carvings, a tiny mermaid preserved in formaldehyde and a ghostly ship in a bottle. When he reached the fireside mantle, his black brows cocked.

William fingered the shrunken head. "Cozy, indeed."

"Have a seat," she offered.

"I've no time for pleasantries."

"Come, Cousin William. There's no need for us to be uncivil." She gestured toward the winged armchair again. "A nightcap?"

He eyed her for a moment before he slumped into the seat, rubbing his brow. Was he tired? Annoyed? Damnation. He would not make her treachery easy.

Madeline stepped toward the liquor cabinet and removed a glass stopper, filling two tumblers with brandy. Keeping her back to the captain, she removed a small vial from a secret compartment and emptied the powdery contents into one of the tumblers.

Would the substance subdue him, she wondered? He was a big man. Tall. Muscular. He might feel some of the drowsy effects . . . or none a'tall. Then what would she do?

Her heart drummed. But she hadn't any more of the drug. It was a potent concoction, though. She'd just have to take the chance and hope—hope a little potion brought down a powerful man.

"Here we are." She swivelled with fanfare. After setting the tainted glass on a small table beside the captain, she took the opposite seat. "Cheers."

"The jewels."

She cleared her throat. "Yes, the jewels. I'm afraid I don't keep them in the house. I've secured the baubles in the bank, to protect them."

He released a long, measured sigh. "I see."

Seconds later he pushed out of the armchair and headed for the door.

"Where are you going?"

"I'm going to tear your cozy house apart until I find the jewels."

She dashed toward the door, blocking his path. "I-I might have a few trinkets tucked in the upstairs rooms. Sit. Drink. I'll fetch them."

"I don't drink, damn it!"

"Bloody hell," she muttered. Was he a prohibitionist? Just her wretched luck.

Suddenly his arms went up on either side of her head, while his nose nearly touched hers. "The jewels, Cousin Maddie. All of them."

His sultry breath caressed her lips, evoking an involuntary shudder. If he hadn't hellfire burning in his eyes, he might even be devilishly handsome. "I can't."

"You won't, you mean?"

"All right, I won't."

His nostrils flared. "You would go to the gallows?"

In a soft voice, she asserted, "If I must."

He pushed away from her, incomprehension in his shadowy gaze. "How could you do this to Lady Amy?"

Another lump gathered in her throat. "I wish my cousin every happiness, but my circumstances are dire."

"A poor excuse. Whatever happened to family?"

"I am doing this *for* family."

"Bullocks."

She fisted her palms. "You are a hard man, Captain Hawkins."

"You've not seen the worst of me."

A chill reverberated down her spine. He was cold. But devoted to his kin. He would do anything to protect his brother and sister-in-law. He was intense, if unemotional. And she had pressed upon *ir*rational sentiments, like flirtation and trickery, instead of more rational ones.

With a better understanding of the man, Madeline took a bold step toward him. "You have not seen the worst of me either, Captain Hawkins." And in a wintry manner, she passed him, pausing behind the writing desk. "I have a grandfather. His name is Sir Richard McNeal."

"The great explorer?"

She removed a folded missive from a locked drawer. "You've heard of him?"

"I've read his tomes."

"Ah, yes, his great adventures to faraway lands. He sailed the world, you know? Searching for treasure. For fame. He sailed beyond the northernmost point of Baffin Island, into the arctic. He had traveled farther than any other explorer at the time. And last year, he died at sea."

"I read his eulogy in the broadsheets."

Madeline settled in an armchair, her legs shaky. "The royalties from his novels provide me with a comfortable income. I am his sole heir. And all this...treasure belongs to me now. I am content, Cousin William. I am not rich. I have no prospects. And I was prepared to spend the rest of my life looking after my grandfather's estate and keeping his memory alive."

"And you need the jewels to save his estate?"

"No, I need the jewels to save my grandfather."

The man frowned. "Save him from what?"

"Pirates." She presented him the letter. "*Real* pirates, Captain Hawkins."

His expression dubious, William reached for the folded paper and unfurled the note.

"Three months ago, this message arrived from the Bahamian Islands," she said, her words now quivering as much as her legs. "A demand for ten thousand pounds in return for my grandfather."

He scanned the few curt lines, concluding brusquely, "A sham."

"I considered it a sham, too. Ne'er-do-wells looking to profit from a grieving granddaughter. But this accompanied the letter." She removed her glove, revealing a slender ring on her middle finger. "Grandfather gave me this ring for my sixteenth year. He said it'd belonged to a princess from the Far East. He always had a tale to tell."

As her heart throbbed, Madeline slipped the glove back over her hand, protecting the keepsake. "I gave him the ring before he set sail. I sensed something dreadful might happen to him during the voyage. 'I promise to return the bauble to ye, lass' he assured me. A year later, I received news of his drowning."

In a startling tender voice, the captain offered, "The pirates might have found his body, the ring still in his possession."

She blinked back tears, her eyes stinging. "Yes, I considered that, as well. But the pirates are demanding ten thousand pounds. An outrageous amount. And a great overestimation of my grandfather's wealth. No doubt *he* is at fault for the ransom price, for he loves to boast, you see? Another reason I believe him alive."

William presented her with a kerchief.

She accepted the surprising gesture of kindness, dabbing at her watery eyes, suspecting the forbidding captain might not be as impassive as she'd first imagined. "You must understand, if there's even the smallest hope of helping my grandfather, I will take it—however dangerous. And if he is dead, and they have his remains, I still want to bring him home. He deserves a proper burial."

The captain dropped back into the opposite armchair, ruminating. "Why didn't you borrow the money?"

"Who could I ask for help? I have no other family."

She rubbed her thumbs together, unsettling memories filling her head. Her admission wasn't entirely true. She had parents, siblings. But she was estranged from the lot of them. Other than Cousin Amy—and her grandfather—Madeline had no other relationship with her kin.

"And my brother, Edmund?" he wondered.

"Cousin Edmund is a good man. But he and Amy have much to worry about, like Gravenhurst."

"Hmm . . . And once you'd amassed the ten thousand pounds worth of jewels? What would you have done?"

"A map accompanied the ransom letter. I would have followed it to the tropical island and made the exchange, of course."

"You? Alone?"

"I can't afford to hire a crew of privateers. And I reasoned, if the pirates wanted future ransom demands to be paid, they wouldn't injure their prisoners. It would ruin their reputation. No one would ever pay them a ransom again."

"A valid point. Business is business, after all."

"Precisely."

After a stretch of agonizing silence, she intervened with, "I haven't much time, Captain Hawkins."

"I understand."

A great sigh of relief. "Oh, thank you for letting me keep the jewels."

"You are not keeping the jewels."

Her heart dropped. "But I must deliver the ransom."

"It's still too dangerous to risk Edmund and Amy's involvement, however indirect. The jewels will be returned to their rightful owners, while the 'thief' will slip through the authority's fingers."

"I see. Your family is more important than mine."

"*Our* family is important, Cousin Maddie. You will surrender *all* the jewels to me—and I will take care of the pirates."

A strange sensation overwhelmed her: a mixture of unfettered hope and intense disbelief. An hour ago he had threatened to hang her. Would he really help her now?

At a loss for words, she blurted out, "What?"

"I have a battle-ready crew who are not afraid to fight slavers or pirates. If your grandfather is still alive, we will rescue him—and destroy the pirates, ransom be damned."

"You would do that?"

"For a price."

She stiffened. A price. Yes, of course. Why else would he make such a generous gesture? Her bewilderment sharpened into a business-like mindset. As his eyes darkened and fixated on her, she prepared herself for the "price" she would pay to rescue her grandfather.

"Name your price, Captain Hawkins."

"William, please. I have a favor to ask of you."

He had dropped all formalities, like captain and cousin, and she braced herself for the "favor" she would owe him . . . for she sensed it was highly personal, indeed.

"Go on," she whispered.

"After I retrieve your grandfather, I want you to deliver a letter to my sister, the Duchess of Wembury."

Her jaw tensed. She waited for the rest of the favor to be revealed, but when he remained mum, she demanded, "Is that all?"

He nodded.

Her brows pinched. She'd anticipated a much heavier burden, a more intimate exchange. His expression, so burning with determination, *still* burning with determination, suggested a very private, even emotional, price.

"I don't understand," she said after a short pause.

"Why not post the letter?"

"I would prefer it travel in safer hands. I would like you to present it to her in person."

"And you can not present the letter yourself?"

"I will not be returning with you to England."

She started. "Why?"

A darkness settled upon his gaze, as if he'd slipped a pair of sunshades over his eyes. "That is my private concern."

"But a ship without a captain?"

"My first lieutenant is a loyal, trustworthy officer. He will see you and your grandfather home to England. As soon as you reach port, you will deliver the letter to my sister. Do we have an agreement?"

Though still unsure about the peculiar circumstances, Madeline wasn't going to lose such an opportunity. "Yes."

"Good." He reached for the brandy. "We set sail at dawn."

"Don't drink that!"

He stopped and glared at her. "Poison?"

"Laudanum."

Slowly he set the glass aside.

CHAPTER 3

Villiam stood aboard the *Nemesis*, watching his crew load supplies: barrels of flour, cheese and salted meats, gunpowder and rum.

One last voyage.

Aye, it was perfect. One last journey to the tropical isles he'd plundered with his father and brothers. One last battle. One last adventure. And if he survived the clash, he'd remain on the island—alone—and await death.

A heaviness lifted from his shoulders. He wouldn't have to confront his family about his wretched demise. He wouldn't have to suffer the humiliation of growing sickly and weak in their presence. He wouldn't have to endure their expressions of pity.

A stout strength filled him, and he heaved an energetic breath.

He turned and scanned the crowded Thames, then lifted his eyes to the foggy cityscape, lingering over the districts where his family lived. His sister would receive his farewell letter, revealing his illness and death. There would be no maudlin gestures of goodbye or weepy embraces. The very thought churned the bile in his belly. It wasn't a proper death for a man, a captain, a pirate.

"Ahoy, Captain."

Her breezy voice hinted at excitement, at the hope of finding her grandfather alive. And if not for her determination to rescue her grandfather, William wouldn't have an honorable reason to weigh anchor and set sail for the Caribbean.

He shifted his gaze and captured sight of Lady Madeline in a simple frock and short tweed coat. Her hair was pinned and stuffed under a matching tweed cap, a few ginger wisps fluttering in the wind. Her cheeks flushed with rosy color. Her eyes danced with faith. And something rent his heart at her beaming optimism. Cold irony, perhaps. That while she searched for life on this journey, he chased death.

"Welcome aboard, Cousin Maddie."

"Maddie, please."

She clutched her carpet bag in both hands, no cumbersome trunks in tow. As she neared him, her smile broadened, and an inadvertent spasm gripped his chest.

"Here." She handed him a paper. "The map."

William unfurled the sheet and eyed the directions, ignoring the quiver in his heart. "I'll plot our course."

"And have you the letter for me?"

"In time." He tucked the map in his pocket. "I've yet to write it."

Before she could make any more uncomfortable inquiries, William signaled his first mate. "Meet Lieutenant Fletcher, Lady Madeline. He will escort you to your cabin."

She paused for a moment, her pupils closing as she pierced him with a curious stare, but she soon bobbed her head. "Thank you, Captain."

As she crossed the deck, William studied her flowing figure and sensed, despite her smart outfit and practical luggage choice, she wasn't going to be a sensible passenger, that his well-ordered ship just might run amok with her onboard.

~ * ~

There was a knock at the door that evening.

"Come in," said William, hunched over the sea chart pinned to the desk. Without averting his attention, he knew who had entered his room. "How do you like your cabin, Maddie?"

"It's very comfortable, thank you."

He had placed her quarters next to his own to protect her, even though he knew his crew would never trouble her, but he still needed to maintain the appearance of propriety, that she was under the captain's charge . . . or perhaps he just didn't trust the woman too far from his sight.

She soon settled beside him. A soft scent swirled in the air, a floral perfume. He suddenly imagined a sultry island filled with bright blooms nestled in a lady's hair. He shut his eyes, the vision unsettling. He wasn't a daydreamer. He wasn't a man who lost focus. Ever.

"Have you plotted our course?" she queried, her voice low.

Slowly he lifted his gaze. Her ginger hair was plaited in a loose braid and draped over her shoulder. Under lamplight, her eyes glowed like embers and a distinct warmth spread throughout his chest.

He pushed the disturbing sensation aside and concentrated on the map. "Aye, we'll travel along the equator and catch the Caribbean current here. It will take us northwest to the Bahamian Islands."

"I'm so excited."

"We're still in the English Channel. There's a long journey ahead."

"I know." She smiled. "Thank you for inviting me to supper."

Again her smile disarmed him. And again he wrestled with the intrusive sentiment that distracted him from his goal—to rescue her grandfather and send both crew and passengers home to England. His invitation to supper was a courtesy, a formal duty every captain performed when hosting civilians aboard ship. And he wouldn't pretend it was anything more than a customary nicety.

Without a word, William walked over to the dining table and pulled out a chair, accustomed to such refinements since retiring from piracy and associating with high society.

Madeline took the offered seat. He joined her at the opposite end of the table, already plated with cooked fare, and removed the silver loche, releasing a cloud of steam and revealing a platter of roasted meats, potatoes and carrots.

He'd every intention of keeping the conversation mundane, when Madeline forked a slice of ham and announced, "I'm grateful for your help, William. It's a good thing you didn't drink the laudanum cocktail."

He arched a brow before serving himself. "What would you have done if I'd taken the laudanum?"

"Packed up the jewels and boarded the first ship to the Caribbean."

"And left me on the floor?"

Her eyes danced with merriment. "You would have roused in time — but long after I was gone."

William shook his head. After so many years at sea, he had learned to listen to his instincts, to spot danger leagues away. And his instincts told him Maddie was trouble. But for once, it wasn't his ship and crew in danger . . . it was him.

"You must think me a fool," she said softly, "hoping for a miracle?"

After a short, uncertain pause, he poured her a glass of wine. "I do not believe in miracles, but there's reason to suspect your grandfather is alive."

Her expression shadowed. "The world darkened when I learned of his death. Other than Cousin Amy, I have no one."

"What happened to the rest of your family?"

She set her wrists on the table, gripping the utensils until her knuckles whitened. "I had an indiscretion with a soldier when I was seventeen. After the scandal broke, I was disowned by my family."

William lifted another brow. In comparison with his own "youthful indiscretions," a fling with a soldier seemed small and undeserving of such severe repudiation. But she was a Lady. A woman. Her position demanded an almost impossible level of deportment.

She loosened her hold of the fork and knife, her

pale features filling with color. "Have I shocked you?"

He snorted. "In my family, we would not have disowned you for such an indiscretion."

"Any why not?"

She had him there. He *should* be shocked by her revelation—if he were a true gentleman.

"I had an unusual upbringing." He shrugged. "I would've sooner crushed the soldier's head and stomped on his bullocks for dishonoring you."

Madeline was about to taste the wine—and paused.

"Have I shocked you?" he mimicked.

She burst into laughter. Musical. Beautiful.

He seized, breathless.

"You sound very much like my grandfather. He wanted to duel with Papa when everyone shunned me." She released a heavy breath. "I would do anything for the devilish old man. He saved my life."

"I understand." Her madcap thievery made more sense to him now. "I would do the same for my kin."

He would also spare them the burden of caring for him as he wasted away. He'd sooner put a bullet in his head than wither into a corpse before their eyes, but suicide would cause an even greater stir and veil the family in ignominy. No, death in battle, at sea, or even on a deserted island was the proper way for a seaman to perish.

Under the bitter circumstances, he was actually fortunate. He had last seen his family during a jubilant ball, leaving him—and them—with the best of memories. And now he had a meaningful way to die.

"William, are you unwell?"

Startled, he snapped, "What do you mean?"

She flinched. "I mean is anything the matter? You've grown so quiet."

As blood thudded through his veins, he sensed another cursed headache pressing on his skull. "No, nothing's the matter," he clipped, even as weakness overpowered him. *Not now*, he railed. *Not in front of her!* His hands shaking, he gritted, "If you'll excuse me, I must finish plotting our course."

He watched her expression turn stony at his uncouth dismissal.

She dropped the utensils on the table and headed for the door. "Of course."

"Take the meal with you," he ordered.

"I'm not hungry."

And she slammed the door behind her.

CHAPTER 4

Madeline was famished. Lamp in hand, she searched the store room for a bit of smoked meat and cheese. She had stormed from the captain's cabin, indignant, confused — and hungry.

As she inspected the barrels, she wondered what the deuces had happened to the man. Had she insulted him? Wounded him? Impossible. If anything, their conversation had been refreshingly honest.

She hooked the lamp to a post and sighed. He seemed a solitary figure, remote, austere. For a moment during supper, he'd revealed a sociable nature, making her laugh. She hadn't laughed since the death of her grandfather. Why had everything gone so awry?

"The boorish, confounding son-of-a — "

Madeline stiffened, her clammy palms curling into fists. As the lamp lilted with the gentle current, shadows played across the room, illuminating, then darkening the supplies. A weighty dampness slithered over her feet, and her heart throbbed as she stared at the wall. *Don't look down!* Of course, her gaze immediately dropped to the ground.

Her eyes widened. Her scream trapped in her throat. She trembled as a *giant* snake glided across the floor, rolling over her toes. A silent prayer shot up to heaven. She waited. And waited. *How long is this bloody vermin?* She didn't even care to know what it was doing in the belly of the ship. She just wanted it *off* her feet.

"Oh, God. Oh, God."

Her voice squeaked like a mouse. At last, the serpent moved off without biting or coiling around her ankles. And the second its slimy tail slinked off her boots, she bolted from the store room, pounding the stairs.

She bounded straight for the captain's cabin. *Bam!* went the door. *Screech!* went the bolt. Safe. She heaved, desperate for breath.

"S-snake!" she finally cried, and with each lungful of air, her heart steadied.

Where was William?

The room was dark. It took her several moments to locate a figure sitting on the bed. In the moonlight, she saw it was the captain, elbows on his knees, head between his hands. His muscular chest gleamed with sweat in the pale light. The bed sheets were tousled around his waist, as if he'd just awakened from a night terror. His feet, bare, were planted a good distance apart, supporting his hunched weight. He was dressed in only his trousers.

She should have knocked. She had startled him, she thought. She could hear his labored breathing from across the cabin. She was about to apologize when a weary voice assured her:

"Don't mind the snake. She looks after the rats."

It wasn't the humdrum way he talked about a monstrous serpent, or the familiar way he referred to it as "she" that troubled Madeline, but the faintness of his voice. He wasn't a tired man just roused from a deep slumber. He was ill.

Slowly she approached him, whispering, "William?"

He remained unmoving, taking in great swells of air, then releasing the breaths like gusts of wind.

She kneeled at his legs and reached for his brow. "You have a fever. I'll fetch a cold compress."

He cinched her wrist, his strength unbreakable, and while his hold wasn't hurtful, it was determined.

"It's not a fever," he returned in an unsettlingly calm voice.

His fingertips then slipped over the inner tendons of her wrist, the tenderness of his touch making her shudder.

Though his tone remained impassive, there was a plaintiveness in his movements. And she sensed something dreadful was amiss.

Madeline remembered their talk over supper, the moment he'd turned cold, brusque . . . when she'd asked him if he was unwell.

The pattering of her heart turned rampant. She searched his arms, his chest for wounds and sighted the scar on his ribcage, just below his heart. "You've been shot!"

"A year ago," he confirmed. "The bullet's still inside me."

"Who shot you?"

"A slaver."

"Is the bullet troubling you?"

"No, it's not the bullet."

"Then *what* is the matter, William?"

His gaze lifted — his angry, frightful gaze. "Leave."

"But — "

"Leave, Maddie."

Her knees remained secured to the floor. "I'm not leaving," she said, defiant. "You need care. And I won't tell the crew, I promise. I know how important it is for a captain to maintain invincibility in the eyes of his tars. My grandfather — "

He cinched her wrist again — and this time it hurt.

"You don't know a damn thing." And he sent her tumbling onto her rump. "Get. Out."

She clenched her trembling jaw, a welter of feeling in her breast — a violent welter of feeling, for when she regained her footing, she slapped him.

For some insufferable reason, tears filled her eyes as she hastened toward the door. She reached for the lock and unarmed the barrier, just as a distant voice murmured:

"I'm not angry with you, Maddie."

She then left the cabin and shut the door.

For a moment, she leaned against the wall, wiping the stinging tears from her eyes. She had heard the truth in his words — that he wasn't furious with her — and for some other intolerable reason, the knowledge comforted her. Yes, she wanted the captain's help to rescue her grandfather. But it was more than the potential loss of his support that had pained her: it was the potential loss of his fellowship.

With a fortifying breath, Madeline regained her

composure. If the captain wasn't livid with her, then with whom? Or with what? And the malady that haunted him?

She intended to find out the answers.

CHAPTER 5

The next morning, Madeline found the captain above deck, robust and forbidding as ever. The crew worked in perfect harmony around him as he gazed across the sea with his spyglass.

The unobtrusive moment allowed her the chance to study him in detail. She noted his dark suede boots and trousers molded his calves and thighs like a second skin, while his white shirt moved fluidly in the breeze. He didn't tie the shirt strings at the nape of his neck, leaving the base of his throat unfettered—and very *un*like the disciplined captain. And that small rebellious gesture sent an unnerving shiver of pleasure through her veins.

She next eyed his fashionable black locks, also ruffled by the wind, the contours of his handsome profile, and the overall confidence his energy exerted. It was clear the tars trusted him. And there was nothing in his rigid manner or cold temperament to suggest anything troubling had happened the night before. Of course, she and William both knew something *had* happened, and she wondered how he would treat her the following morning.

She gathered her courage and slowly crossed the deck. Long before she reached the captain, he sensed her approach and set aside his spy glass, his bright blue eyes turning straight in her direction.

The man's piercing gaze leveled her for a moment, and she paused before regaining her momentum. His uncanny ability to detect the slightest change from a distance both assured and perturbed her. He could not be surprised or set upon by an enemy. A good trait for a captain, she concluded. But he also couldn't be approached by a friend. A poor trait for a man, she thought.

"Good morning, Lady Madeline," he said in a polite, but flat tone. "How did you sleep?"

She hadn't expected an acknowledgment of their curious encounter the other night, but she also hadn't expected his outright dismissal of it. He looked at her with the composure of a sober, able-bodied seaman, and for a second, she doubted anything unusual had occurred. Had she dreamed the entire incident?

But her rump still throbbed with tenderness, and she knew she hadn't dreamed a bit of it. The man was savvy, she admired. He had almost hypnotized her into believing nothing frightful had taken place in the late hours of the night.

But Madeline would not be dissuaded.

"Not too shabby," she returned. "I'm still gaining my sea legs."

His eyes impaled her with a mesmerizing force, and if his conduct toward the ship and crew remained much the same, his attitude toward *her* had noticeably shifted. She wanted to assure him—

again—she would not reveal his secret to the tars. She wanted him to trust her *with* his secret, whatever it was. And he must have guessed her thoughts, for his sharp voice offered:

"There's ginger in the galley."

And again he dismissed her.

Madeline wasn't flustered this time. She had a better understanding of the complicated man. And while his brush-off made it clear he didn't want her poking into his private life, she still intended to search for answers. Not out of nosiness. But out of concern. The man needed her help. It was the only certainly on their perilous voyage.

~ * ~

William heard laughter. Palms-slapping-knees sort of guffaws. He followed the sound of the irritating amusement to the poop, where he stilled.

There on the steps was Madeline. Her plaited hair had come loose in the wind, the long ginger wisps flickering like candle flames. Her eyes, bright with merriment, glowed in the fading light of dusk. The joy teeming from her was brilliant and bone-crushing. For all her hardships, she had not lost her passion for life, for hope. And an inexplicable, even dangerous, desire pulled him toward her radiance.

His chest tightened. He resisted the intense draw. It would only lead to . . . death. His death. His inevitable, fucking death.

As he dragged in a great swell of air, he cursed himself for being weak, for wistfully wishing for impossible desires. He had a mission to complete: to die with honor. He wasn't aboard ship to get embroiled with a woman, especially a woman with whom he had no future.

William remained in the shadows, watching his tars around Madeline, splitting their breeches with laughter. Whatever she had told them had captured their mirth with howling hilarity. And he knew then his well-ordered ship *would* run amok with her onboard.

"Tell us another, lass," from his first lieutenant.

It annoyed William that his first lieutenant was participating in the discord. It burned his blood to hear him call her the affectionate "lass" instead of Lady Madeline, as was proper.

"All right," she said. "Here's a frightening tale that'll turn your whisker's white."

The men hushed in unadulterated silence.

"In seventeen eighty-three, my grandfather was part of an expedition to the Bahamian islands, transporting the very first English colonists. He'd taken the post for one reason: to find the Fountain of Youth. As a boy, he'd heard tales about Ponce de Leon's discovery of a mysterious island, where the water possessed healing powers. But there were hundreds of islands in the area, and it soon became clear to him it would take a lifetime to search them all. After several, fruitless years at sea, he ordered his ship back to England, but before leaving Caribbean waters, he had a strange encounter.

"One moonlit night, my grandfather was on deck, stargazing. He heard a soft voice singing a hymn. It sounded like a female voice, but there were no women aboard his ship. He searched the horizon, expecting to see the bright white sails of another vessel. The horizon was empty. He called for his spyglass and more closely examined the waters. He soon saw a shocking sight—a woman floating in the water."

"Crikey!" cried the men.

"He shouted 'man overboard' and heroically jumped ship, swimming toward the drowning woman. She must have fallen from another ship, he thought. As he stroked toward her, he prayed he'd reach her in time. Her voice sounded very weak. His crew, meanwhile, bustled into action, bringing light and readying a small craft to scoop up their captain and the castaway.

"As my grandfather reached the woman, he prepared to grab her, but just then, she turned and swatted him—with her tail!"

The men uttered a collective gasp—and a few curses, as well.

"She hit him so hard, he almost blacked out. A second later, she burrowed her claws into his arms and pushed him underwater. She wrapped her body around him like a snake and attempted to drown him. If his shipmates hadn't rowed out to save him, he would have died. The sailors beat the creature with their oars until she released my grandfather. She screamed in an unearthly voice before disappearing under the waves."

"Gor, I hope I never meet the likes," uttered a lone voice.

"I was a girl when my grandfather first told me the story. He even showed me the scars on his arms, where the siren had pierced him. He believed she'd wanted him for her supper. It was his most harrowing escape!"

A great cacophony exploded then, some men claiming to have seen the creature, others crossing themselves in the hopes of never coming across such a beast.

William cleared his throat — loudly.

The sailors stood at attention. After a moment of awkward silence, the first lieutenant shouted "resume your duties."

As boots trampled the deck in haste, William eyed Madeline — and crooked his finger . . .

When he entered his cabin, Maddie was at his heels.

"Is something the matter?" she queried in a benign voice, shutting the door.

"Aye," he snapped. "I don't want you distracting my crew."

"But —"

"We're in open waters, and there are many threats. I need my men alert, watching for storms, other ships, even fantastical *mermaids* who might drag them to the seabed for a meal."

"Aye, Captain," she returned sheepishly. "It won't happen again. I'm just grateful for the tars' service. I wanted them to know my grandfather, to know the man they're risking their lives to save."

"My men serve *me*, not you. And they're risking their lives to save your grandfather because I'm paying them to do it. Do you understand?"

"Yes, Captain."

"Good." He went over to the sea chart, sensing another damnable headache. "Now get out."

CHAPTER 6

Madeline settled on the bed and pressed her ear against the wall. Was that a man's groan? Or the ship boards creaking? Damn. She couldn't hear a blasted thing.

Scrambling off the mattress, she snatched a water glass from the table. She cupped one end of the glass to her ear and pressed the other to the wall. The funneled sound was stronger, but still incoherent. She sighed, slumping on the bed.

William had booted her from his room—again—vexed with her "distracting" behavior, but he'd also evinced the same haggard expression from the previous night. Was he ill? Did he need her help?

He would never ask his tars for assistance, whatever his mysterious ailment. He would never seek her support, either, she reckoned, no matter how many times she vowed to keep his secret.

"Stubborn ass," she muttered.

Still, she couldn't leave him in distress. She considered barging into his room, but worried he'd throw her overboard in frustration. She next considered a polite rap on the door and an innocent inquiry into his health, but she was sure he'd tell her to bugger off.

No, her last and best resort was to sneak into his room while he was sleeping and check on him. At least, then, she'd be assured of his wellbeing without an unpleasant confrontation.

Madeline had a few hours ahead of her before implementing her plan. The oil lamp on the table still burned, and she settled between the pillows, too tired to rouse and turn down the flame.

Instead, she faced the warm glow, closed her eyes and imagined the lush garden on her family estate in the summertime. Strange how childhood memories comforted her now . . .

Madeline fingered the velvety soft rose petals from her mother's prized stock, inhaled their intoxicating perfume. Such sweetness always made her drowsy and she rested under an oak tree.

Suddenly an acorn tapped her on the head. She looked up to find a boy in the branches, grinning down at her. She turned as red as her mother's roses before she scrambled up the tree after the jackanapes. He taunted her as she climbed. And she was good and ready to clobber him when she reached the canopy. But the boy lost his footing . . . and fell.

His descent was slow. She watched every moment in horror, unable to scream for help. He hit the ground, his body broken and bloody. Frantic, she clambered down the tree and rushed to his side.

The grass was stained with blood, so much blood. It pooled at her ankles. She covered her head to protect her eyes from the smoke and shrapnel, to protect her nose from the stench of sulphur, to protect her ears from the blasts of cannons and muskets. She kneeled beside the boy. But he was dead.

Madeline sobbed. Blood dissolved into fire. Fire turned into smoldering ash. At last she realized she was in bed, far away from the battlefield. She tossed aside the covers and breathed long and deep.

Blimey, what a nightmare. No, not a nightmare. A memory. Many memories mashed together, both wonderful and gruesome. It was not the first time she'd had such a patchwork dream. It would not be the last.

As her heart steadied, she eased off the feather tick. What time was it? she wondered and glanced at the clock on the wall. Almost midnight. William would be asleep at such an hour, she reasoned. What if sneaking into his room disturbed him? He needed rest. But if something else had happened to him? Something unfortunate?

She raked her teeth over her bottom lip. She looked at the clock again. A quarter after twelve. She let out a frustrated sigh and marched into the passageway.

After her frightening dream, she needed to see the captain more than ever. Still, her feet dragged as she approached the man's door. And when she reached it, her belly tightened.

She tested the latch. Unlocked. Slowly she pushed the barrier and peeked inside the cabin.

It took her several moments to adjust to the faint light, but she soon spotted William on the bed, his legs arched in a twisted pose, his forearm draped over his brow.

Her heart cramped with compassion. Was he in pain? Or just asleep? Surely, he was asleep. And she turned away. But a relentless voice nagged: *what if he's hurt?*

Yes, what if?

Madeline huffed again, gathered her wits and walked toward the bed.

As she neared the slumbering figure, she noted his teeth clenched together. His shirt, half unlaced, revealed a wall of muscle, covered in tufts of dark hair, and she watched his chest expand with every hard breath.

She kneeled at the bedside, so close to him, and rested her palm over his throbbing heart. She sensed his breath stirring the fine hairs on her wrist and gasped softly at the titillating feel of gooseflesh tightening across her arm, her whole body. But she didn't pull her hand away. She left it splayed across the center of his breast, counting the powerful beats beneath his shirt.

Her own heart roared, and the longer she kept her hand in place, the more the organ boomed. Her touch lingered another tense moment before she slipped her hand away, and though it was an improper reaction, she was unsettled to lose his pulse.

Soon her fingertips traced his sternum, spread across his clavicle bone and down over his pectoral muscle. He flinched under her probing touch. His breathing hastened. So alive, she thought, much assured.

The heat radiating through his shirt very nearly scorched her palm, yet she didn't take her hand off his body. She couldn't. Mesmerized. Her own pulse thumped in her head, and disoriented, she almost missed the hoarse "Maddie" that scraped between his lips.

"What the hell are you doing?" he growled.

Madeline snapped upright, gasping for air. "Forgive me. I—I wanted to make sure you were all right."

"Bloody hell, you're incorrigible."

"Thank you.

"That wasn't a compliment."

And he rolled his arm away, revealing his smoky eyes and miserable expression. Flustered, she scurried toward the wash basin and moistened a towel. She felt wholly wanton. Her fingers flexed as she remembered the captain's hammering heartbeat, the heat, the life teeming from him, his uneven breath on her skin, so arousing.

She turned away, cheeks burning. What the devil had possessed her to touch him in such a familiar manner?

The nightmare. The nightmare had unsettled her. Her nerves thrummed even now. It was the only logical explanation for her shameful behavior.

"You should have a doctor aboard ship," she chastised, regaining her composure and crossing the room. She placed the cool compress over his fevered brow. "I wouldn't have to look after you, then."

"I didn't ask for your help."

"But you need it."

He grabbed the compress and dropped it on the floor. "Get out, Maddie."

She was bloody tired of hearing him order her "out" of his room, "out" of his life and snatched the towel off the floor, plopping it back on his head. "If there was a doctor aboard ship, I'd leave."

"There *is* a doctor," he verily snarled. "My youngest brother, Quincy."

"Well, where is he?"

Then grumbling, "He's not joining us on this voyage."

"I see." She placed her arms akimbo. "And you're not joining us on our return trip to England. Did you quarrel with your family? Is that why you're spending time apart from them?"

"No," he gritted. "Now get—"

"Out. I know." She toted a chair to the side of the bed and dropped into the seat, arms folded under her breasts. "I shan't leave unless you carry me out."

"Fine."

Madeline shrieked as he hoisted off the mattress.

~ * ~

William groaned. A merciless pressure squeezed both sides of his skull, borrowing into his temples and stomping his brain so hard, his eyeballs pulsed alongside his heartbeat. He was uneven on his feet and dropped back on the edge of the bed. In the moonlit murk, he waited, impotent, for the agony to pass.

As soon as he recovered from his headache, he'd strangle the impossible woman. Damn her. Damn her for being here. Damn her for seeing him like this. So weak.

Stonewalled, he released a relenting breath and crashed against the pillow. "Hide," he warned her. "Hide from me when I've healed."

"Don't be such a grump." After retrieving the towel again, she mopped his brow. "You would never hurt me. I'm family."

"So?"

"So, you would never hurt your family. I know *that* about you."

The same disagreeable, unwelcomed, protective instinct came over him at her decisive assertion.

"You're just acting the part of a tyrant," she went on, "to conceal the pain."

Her precise recognition of his motives perturbed him even more. He prayed his crew wasn't half as mindful as the tenacious Lady Madeline.

"How long have you suffered from vertigo?" she wondered in a quiet voice.

He shut his eyes, ignoring the storm in his breast. "It isn't vertigo."

"A headache, then?"

"Hmm."

Headache. Blood loss. Frailty. Then death.

He grimaced at the inevitable procession of grisly symptoms: symptoms he couldn't fight, much less destroy. And a rage billowed inside him. It crushed his ribs, took his breath away.

"Here." She tipped a glass to his lips. "Drink."

"A laudanum cocktail?"

"Sorry, no."

"Damn," he muttered as he downed the water.

He heard a faint chuckle, the same musical laughter. Such a beautiful sound had a reviving effect on him. But soon the discomfort returned, worsened. His thoughts twisted with an ugly truth: in a few months, he wouldn't hear such lyrical laughter, the warmth of it, the joy . . .

His teeth clenched again. He sensed the blood

pooling at his nose.

William seized the compress and soaked up the blood before she noticed it. As his heart gathered strength, he barked, "Out!"

She snorted. "I shan't leave unless you carry me out."

Her repetitive rebuff gnawed at his innards. He would *not* permit her — or anyone else — to watch him fall apart.

He tossed the compress aside. "I see you're going to be a bloody nuisance." And he cradled the back of her head, wrenching her toward his mouth. "Do not come back here again, Maddie."

He kissed her — hard — for good measure.

Shit, that was a mistake. The woman didn't screech *or* struggle. No, she opened her damnable lips and *let* him ravish her. And he ached. He ached for her. For more of her.

William took her deeper into his mouth and groaned, low in his throat. Her every thrust, so bold, chased away the nightmare in his soul. He had lived with death for so long. And for so long, he had denied himself the pleasure of life. Such sweet pleasure, like a woman's intimate touch.

He threaded his hand through her mussed hair, holding her. The blood in his veins surged with want. His muscles throbbed for . . .

She gasped when he pushed her away.

No, he wouldn't take her. He wouldn't let the rough and wild moment spiral out of control. Was he mad? Inviting such danger into his life? What the hell would've happened if he'd bedded the woman?

He wouldn't be so irresponsible. Not now. Not at

the end of his life. And since *she* hadn't any sense about the matter, he'd have to gather the strength to resist her . . . but as he stared into her bewitching eyes and listened to the sound of her hastened breathing, the sound of her unfulfilled longing, he wasn't sure where in the hell he'd find the power to resist her—especially knowing she desired him in return.

Girding his muscles, he lifted from the bed and took hold of her arm, dragging her toward the door. "If you come back here again, I'll throw you in the brig." And he shoved her into the passageway.

William then leaned against the door, his head throbbing, spinning. Somehow, he could *feel* her standing on the other side of the barrier, her soul in just as much turmoil. And the danger he'd dreaded closed in on him. It uprooted his logic, his reason, his impenetrable control. It left a gaping void of chaotic emotions that threatened to destroy him.

Suddenly, an apprehension worse than death filled him . . . the thought of caring for Maddie.

CHAPTER 7

Madeline leaned against the starboard rail. The cloudland stretched on forever. The heavens billowed in the distance and pulsed with electric light, but the storm traveled in the opposite direction. Still, a heavy wind pressed against her back, disentangling her plaited hair. And much like her emotions, the wisps fluttered at wayward angles.

William had ignored her for several days—and he'd bolted his door every night, the cheek of the man. She wasn't a seducer, chasing after the hapless captain. How dare he insinuate such a thing! *He* had kissed her. Aye, she'd returned the buss. Enjoyed it. Savored it, even. Yet . . .

Her fickle indignation turned into longing as she remembered the hot feel of his lips, the passion coursing through his blood, the unfettered desire he'd released, and she wondered what had ever made her think him an unfeeling brute.

She reached for her mouth, touched her lips, shuddering, the sensation of pleasure still there . . . the want still there. Perhaps the captain was wise to lock his door, she mused.

Madeline sighed. Apart from the unexpected kiss, their relationship was simple. A business deal, really. An exchange of services. William would rescue her grandfather. She would deliver a letter to his sister, the duchess. A straightforward, uncomplicated transaction. Was she breaching their bargain?

She considered steering clear of him as he'd requested — well, demanded — but the thought of leaving him alone, in pain, repulsed her, and she quickly rejected the idea. He deserved her support. She wouldn't turn away from him. She wouldn't abandon him in need, like her family had abandoned her. His pride was just an obstacle. And she'd defeated many obstacles in the past.

"Look out!"

Her daydream shattered — but the warning had come too late.

A large sack of flour being lowered into the galley by a pulley came crashing down, clipping her backside, knocking her off her feet . . . and sending her over the rail.

Madeline screamed as she plummeted toward the water, crashing into the icy surf with such force, her chest seized, taking her breath away. It was several disorienting moments in the dark and frigid water before she surfaced, struggling against the weight of her wet garment which threatened to drag her to the seabed.

She kicked and paddled, as her grandfather had taught her many years ago, arduously swimming back toward the *Nemesis*. She ignored the panicked cries aboard ship and bellowing curses distracted her, but then she heard a loud splash.

From the ring of roiling bubbles surfaced a sailor. William.

He stroked toward her at breakneck speed and clinched her waist, dragged her back to the rig.

The rope ladder was lowered.

William thrust her against the wooden rings. "Climb," he ordered.

Her fingers numb, she grasped the rings and scaled the ladder, every step slow and shaky, but with the captain right behind her, pushing her onward, she finally reached the top deck.

Several hands grabbed her and hoisted her over the rail. A wool blanket draped her shoulders. A mug of rum was pressed into her hands.

Shivering, Madeline gulped the rum, needing the fortifying drink, her mind in a tizzy, her heart slamming into her ribs like a battering ram.

As soon as the captain boarded the ship, the tars collectively separated from her, their expressions wary. And with good reason. A sidelong glance revealed the captain's livid features. She'd be spooked, too, if confronted with such a glare. She had never seen the man more incensed—not even with her.

And though her tumbling overboard had been a happenstance, she sensed the crew would pay dearly for the accident. But before any vicious reprimands passed between his lips, William's features changed, crippled.

Madeline sensed the moment vertigo gripped him, the moment a surge of pain wracked his head. She had seen that expression many times before and realized the man was about to collapse—in front of his crew—and not from a valiant bullet wound earned in the heat of battle, but from scooping a slight chit out of the calm sea.

There was no greater defeat, no greater humiliation for a captain than to fall apart in front of his men, and Madeline quickly stepped at William's side, feigning distress.

Her arms went around his waist, her temple rested on his chest, and she coughed, then whispered, "Thank you for escorting me back to my cabin, Captain. I need rest."

He remained taut, desperate to maintain his composure. She tugged at him, encouraging him to lean on her and *move*. As he hobbled, she stumbled, too, making it appear as though the captain was supporting *her* floundering steps.

The crew parted, creating a channel, their heads hung in dismay as she and the captain passed in complete silence. Fortunately, William's reticence prompted guilty sentiments instead of suspicious ones. As far as she could observe, the tars believed their captain too enraged to speak, not ill, and that was all she wanted them to think for now.

As soon as she reached the captain's cabin, she helped him toward the bed where he finally collapsed, his features contorted. He was shaking, his eyes shut tight, and blood was seeping from his nose.

She stifled an alarmed cry and kneeled beside the bed, taking his hand. "What can I do?"

"Nothing," he gritted. "It'll pass, as always."

She fetched a towel and returned to his bedside, mopping the blood. "Oh, William."

"You . . . all right?" he stuttered, floating in and out of consciousness.

"I'm fine," she assured him, squeezing his hand again.

"Almost . . . lost . . . you."

"No, I can swim. My grandfather taught me as a child."

"Almost . . . drowned."

"No," she repeated more forcefully. "I can swim, William. I'm alive." And she bussed his quivering lips as proof. "I'm alive."

He blacked out then.

Madeline slumped on her heels, tears rolling down her cheeks. She listened to his haggard breathing for a few frustrating minutes before she pushed aside her grief. She had work to do. And though she wasn't a trained nurse, she had enough knowledge about basic care to help him through his latest episode.

After she'd changed into dry clothes, Madeline returned to the captain's cabin and bolted the door. She first divested his wet clothes using a knife she'd found wedged in his boot. He was too heavy for her to maneuver, so she'd simply sliced the garments, yanked off his boots, then covered him with a series of blankets.

He trembled still, from pain, not fever, and she couldn't watch him writhe in discomfort without resorting to bloody tears.

After a thoughtful pause, she crawled across the bed, lifted the covers, and snuggled beside his naked body. She crooked one arm and nestled her hand under her chin, stretching her other arm across the breadth of his chest.

His warmth, his heartbeat comforted her, even if it didn't offer him much solace . . . or perhaps her proximity soothed him after all, for he soon settled and breathed with greater strength, his rhythm even.

"Oh, William," she whispered once more, her cheek pressed against his shoulder. "What ails you?"

But she suspected she might not want to learn the truth anymore.

CHAPTER 8

*M*adeline found herself on a roaring battlefield, ducking whizzing bullets and dodging fleeing soldiers. As the stinging smoke cleared, she spotted a body splayed in the trampled grass.

William.

She ran toward him, screamed his name, but he remained unmoving, bleeding from the chest. She pressed her hands over the bullet wound at his heart, desperate to stymie the blood flow, but the fiery fluid gushed between her fingers unchecked.

"No," she cried. "Don't die. Please don't die!"

With a twitch, Madeline awakened, her heart pounding, her lungs starved for air. It took her several frantic moments to regain her poise and realize it was another dream. But what was William doing on the battlefield? Dying?

She shuddered at the perturbing thought — and seized when a large hand squeezed her hip. There was a heavy arm draped around her body, and a male chest tucked under her cheek. A very naked male chest.

Madeline stifled a groan. She had fallen asleep in the captain's bed — *on* the captain. She hadn't intended to find herself in the compromising position. She'd meant to leave the bed before he'd recovered from his delirium, but her own bones had ached from the fall, and the warmth of the mattress, the man's flesh had been an irresistible comfort.

Her cheeks burned, but not with shame. The quiet intimacy suited her after such a night terror, and she longed to remain in the harmonious moment. But the captain had also threatened to throw her in the brig if he ever found her in his cabin again, much less his bed, and the harmony between them fractured as she wondered what sort of mood he was in—benevolent or punishing.

She turned her head and peeked at him, meeting his smoldering gaze, and another shudder wracked her body, so sultry and titillating. He sensed it. His arm tightened around her. And his eyes burned ever hotter.

Something had changed between them. She found herself staring into the eyes of a very different man. A man who had lowered his guard. And as she delved into the pools of his beautiful blue irises, a wealth of feeling overwhelmed her, frightened her, even.

"Are you all right?" he asked, voice gravelly with sleep.

"I-I'm fine. I had a nightmare."

He lifted his other hand and brushed a tousled lock away from her moist brow. "And the fall?"

"Oh, the fall. Yes, I'm all right."

Madeline uttered a soft squeak as the hand on her hip shifted, covered her rump, and hoisted her up the length of his frame until they were nose to nose . . . lips to lips.

"Tell me the truth, Maddie."

The truth? The truth about what? That his breath tickled her sensitive skin until she wanted to take his mouth and ravish him? That his hand, still braced on her arse, shot waves of sensual desire though her feverish blood? That her nightmare had opened a new chapter in her life, where she now feared for William's survival?

There was too much to confess, too much to lose . . . and much to gain with the truth.

But she would give him her truth, she decided at last.

"Touch me, William."

His breath hitched. "Maddie—"

"I need you. And I think you need me, too."

As his muscles stiffened in resistance, she stroked his cheek. "For tonight," she rasped. "Just for tonight."

Her own muscles firmed with want. And fear. He might still reject her, toss her from the room, but she wanted the hurt in her soul relieved, the loneliness gone—for a while, at least.

He trembled a tense moment longer—then gripped her tresses and pulled her in for a kiss.

When their lips touched, her heart spasmed. His kiss wasn't punishing, a deterrent to keep her away. For the first time, he'd opened for her, trusted her, and his buss was welcoming, tender, and, oh, so hungry.

Madeline sighed with sweet relief and dropped her own guard. As his fingers grazed the length of her hair and slipped over the knobs of her spine, she shivered, and soon found herself tumbling in bed, being pressed against the mattress.

Her troubles were quickly forgotten as he ministered gentle kisses, pecking her cheeks, her nose before tending to her flushed lips once more. He handled her in a light, even delicate manner. Afraid she'd break in his hold? Or perhaps he just cherished the moment, cherished her?

Her heart jerked. A want filled her. The primal need to be adored, revered. She'd neglected her desires far too long, bound by guilt and regret. But for one night, she would pretend she had no scandalous past, that she was deserving of intimacy. She imagined she was alone in the world with William, the only two creations on earth, joining for the first time. She would not hide her body or mind or soul from him.

As soon as he sensed her submission, he heaved with unfettered emotion—and his kisses turned rich, more sensual and invading, taking everything she offered, and giving much dreamed of pleasure in return. And healing. She hadn't realized the breadth of her suffering until pure delight swarmed the void in her heart, and she sobbed with joy.

William's kisses gained ferocity. His fingers curled into her dress, clumping the thin material, yanking it off her shoulders. The linen stretched across her breasts. She heard the fine threads splitting apart before he rent the fabric.

Her heart jumped. She was moist with sweat, covered in quivering gooseflesh. She dragged in a much-needed breath as he broke away from her mouth, his hot lips hungering at her throat and down her breastbone. He bussed her breasts, first one then the other, before he took a nipple into his mouth.

Madeline gasped. Her whole body arched as he sucked her areola, drawing her deeper into his ravenous mouth. She clasped his hair, holding him tighter against her flesh. And when he flicked his tongue across the sensitive nub, she cried "*yes*," choking on the word. His tongue circled and laved, provoking more shouts of insatiable longing.

With a guttural growl, he soon settled between her thighs, hooked an arm under her knee—and slipped into her.

Her spine pitched as unhindered arousal coursed through her very marrow. She panted at the full length of him, then moaned, over and over, as he rocked inside her, so slow, like a rhythmic dance. Her quim throbbed for more.

"William," she cried, bucking her hips. "Harder."

She clutched his wet backside, lifting her rump, and he grunted with each swift penetration, thrusting deeper still, his every stroke rough yet tender until a savage need pooled within her, demanded gratification, and violent release wracked her bones, her muscles thrumming in ecstasy.

She heard a desperate groan as he orgasmed inside her, and then the world went quiet in the euphoric afterglow of lovemaking.

It was several breathless minutes before he separated from her, sated, and buried his mouth in the crook of her neck. Shaking, she curled into his protective embrace.

"Thank you," she whispered.

"Damn, woman." His thigh anchored between

her legs. A finger soon followed, sliding into her still sensitive quim. "I will always give you what you want. Don't ask me for it. Don't beg me for it. And don't ever thank me for it. Do you understand?"

"Aye," she gasped, holding him for balance, moving her hips to match his seductive undulations.

"Then take," he said in a harsh, almost angry voice. "Take anything you want from me. Take everything from me, if it pleases you."

"I will," she vowed, unsure why he'd made such a sacred offer, but it was clear "just one night" wouldn't be enough, not for either of them.

Her thoughts in an uproar, she dismissed the confusion and listened to his hypnotic voice resounding in her head: *Take anything you want from me. Take everything from me, if it pleases you.*

She obeyed. For once. And it was under his devoted, carnal ministrations she orgasmed again—and again—before blissful satisfaction turned into blissful sleep.

CHAPTER 9

W hy do you keep a snake aboard ship?"
William almost nicked his throat
shaving when he looked at Madeline's
refection in the mirror, her supple arse so damn
tempting in the morning light. He watched her as
she slipped into the frock he'd fetched from her
room, buttoning the front length, covering her
beautiful breasts.

She then collected the dress he'd rent, inspecting
it, perhaps wanting to repair it, and he stifled a
groan at the memory of their heady night together,
and how he'd lost control of his senses — something
he had never done before.

"Why not keep a cat to look after the rats?" she
wondered.

William put away the straight razor before he
sliced his throat, unable to concentrate and maintain
a steady grip with her in the same cabin. He dunked
his hands in the bowl of hot water and washed his
face before toweling his semi-sheared cheeks.

"The snake belongs to my eldest brother, James.
He found her in Jamaica many years ago. But after
he married . . ."

"Ah, his wife would have nothing to do with it. A sensible woman."

Aye, sensible. His sister-in-law, Sophia, loathed the serpent, which was named after her, and had tried on several occasions to lop off its head. James had given William the yellow boa to protect its life. But William wouldn't be able to look after the reptile much longer.

"I intend to release her in the Bahamas," he said, thoughtful.

"Good."

Madeline tamed her long brown hair, braiding and twisting the unruly curls, pinning the tresses in place, and he observed the simple ritual with intimate pleasure.

"I hate wending through the ship, fearing it'll swallow me whole."

A very *un*subtle complaint.

"I have a terrarium." He latched the shaving kit, putting it away. "I'll place her inside the habitat until we reach the islands."

Her arms stealthy slipped around his naked waist. He stiffened. She had sneaked up behind him. But how? He was always alert. Yet with Maddie . . .

And how strange, he thought, that a surprise embrace wasn't so perturbing? At least, not from her.

She grazed one hand across his ribs and backside, tracing the line of his spine with her fingertip. He shuddered at the sensuous touch. Her warm lips pressed between his shoulder blades, and he shut his eyes at the arousing gesture, at the mounting desire in his blood . . . desire he wouldn't be able to restrain much longer.

"Maddie, I have to go above deck."

"I'm not asking, Captain." Her hand dropped to his arse, scraping his buttocks. He gritted as her slender fingers raked his muscles, exploring . . . craving . . . torturing him even more. "I'm taking."

He grunted in defeat, turned and latched onto her smoldering gaze. Her bold demand disarmed him. Aye, he'd given her permission to take as much as she wanted from him, but to feel and hear her yearning almost crippled him. She coveted life like no other woman he had ever met, and he was irrepressibly drawn to her unbound passion.

William cast off the shadow of death that always trailed after him and pushed her against the table.

"Be gentle, Captain. I don't have many dresses left."

Her sultry chastisement weakened him even more. Rucking her skirt over her hips, he hoisted her onto the table.

"Open for me," he ordered. "Wide."

Blood rushed to her cheeks, her full lips. She lifted her knees, her breathing swift and shallow. His own lungs expanded with desperate mouthfuls of air as he stepped between her splayed thighs, unfastened his trousers—and thrust into her.

Madeline released a sensual moan and dropped her head back in abandon.

"Is this deep enough for you?" he growled, buried in the tight folds of her wet quim.

She gasped. "Yes."

He bumped her hips, quick and rough. "Is this hard enough for you?"

"Yes," she cried. "Yes!"

"Do you want more, Maddie?"

"Yes," she pleaded, gripping the table for balance as he pumped inside her with swift, piercing strokes. "Don't stop, William."

The wood joints of the table creaked and stomped as he pounded into her, and she arched her body, drawing him more fully into her womb. It was madness. Sweet madness. And when he sensed her muscles spasm in orgasm, and her shouts of pleasure carry throughout the cabin, he released his seed, burrowing into her one last blessed time.

She almost dropped on the table, so faint, but he captured her in his arms, trembling after such intense sex.

"Are you satisfied?" he murmured into her ear.

"For now," she whispered with a sly smile.

In the serene silence that followed, he cradled her in his embrace, inhaled her divine scent, listened to her labored breathing, and he suddenly ached to never let her go. In that moment, he realized he was doomed, that she had a hold over him like a fabled siren — an unbreakable hold — and he cursed himself for letting her get so close to his heart. The shadow of death returned, but now it trailed after both of them — for soon he would leave her. Forever.

But not today, he thought in defiance. Not today. And he searched for a reason to remain with her in the perfect moment.

He rubbed her spine and bussed her salty throat. "You had a nightmare last night," he said offhand. "Tell me about it?"

And though it was dangerous growing even closer to her, the temptation was just too much to resist.

She wrapped her legs around his waist, keeping him near, fingering his hair in wayward fashion.

"I dream about the past sometimes, about a boy. He was the youngest son of my father's steward. And such a devil. At every turn, he yanked my hair, kicked dirt at my dress, tossed acorns at my head. I had him whipped on several occasions."

William chuckled.

"He deserved it," she defended herself. "He hadn't a proper bone in his body."

"Too love sick, I suppose."

Her muscles stiffened. "Aye, too love sick. I learned his true feelings for me later in life. And at sixteen, I found myself feeling much the same toward him."

He caressed her back, comforting her. "What happened?"

"He joined a regiment."

"The soldier? Your 'youthful indiscretion'?"

"Aye. At nineteen, he ascended to the position of an officer. When his orders took him to Belgium, he asked me to come with him, to elope."

"You're a widow?"

"No, we never married. I followed him to Belgium with every intention of becoming his wife, but when he was captured in battle and imprisoned at Verdun, in Eastern France, I—I changed my mind about staying with him. I was permitted to live with him at Verdun, like the wives of other officers, but the lodgings were poor, the company unsociable." She ended weakly, "I wanted to go home."

"I understand, Maddie."

"I abandoned him."

"At sixteen," he consoled her. "A child."

"A stupid child."

He heard the tears in her voice and tightened his embrace, determined to soothe her.

"Charles was devastated," she said in a shaky voice. "I was allowed to leave Verdun in a ransom exchange with a group of officers, but Charles remained imprisoned, his rank too low to be worth much money.

"Later, I learned he'd tried to escape. He was shot in the back. He died . . . calling my name. If I had stayed with him—"

"You might be dead, too."

She hiccupped. "What?"

He thumbed her chin, lifting her watery eyes, and stroked her chafed skin. "If Charles had died in prison from injury or illness or hunger, you would've been alone, the guards' whore, tortured. It's all right, Maddie, that you returned home. And lived."

She cupped the back of his hand, holding it against her moist and fevered flesh. "I wasn't welcomed home, though. It all still seemed for nothing."

"It wasn't for nothing." He bussed her briny tears, drinking in her sorrow. "If you hadn't lived, I would never have found you."

She offered him a half smile, then pulled him in for a long, hard kiss, and it took all his energy to separate from her before she blinded his good sense once more.

"Where are you going?" she wondered.

He pulled a shirt over his chest and fastened his trousers. "I have to check on the crew, the ship." And he still had that letter to write to his sister. Shoving his feet into his boots, he then combed his fingers through his mussed hair.

Madeline hopped off the table, her skirt fluttering around her ankles. "And your headache?"

He headed for the door. "Gone."

"You're welcome."

He hardened. "I beg your pardon?"

"I seem to be the cure for what ails you, Captain."

A raging fire burned in his belly. "You are a dangerous woman, Maddie."

"Thank you," she returned in a hushed tone.

He opened the door, then glanced at her sidelong. "That wasn't a compliment."

CHAPTER 10

Over the next fortnight, as the air grew sultry and the waters warmer, Madeline spent each night in the captain's bed. It was an unspoken arrangement between them, where neither asked, nor invited, nor teased the other in a flirtatious dance.

At ten o'clock every evening, she would enter his room — and his arms.

He waited for her. Always. At times, the cabin was dark, the man in wretched pain. And she held him through the night in silence. Other times, under resplendent lamplight, he took her in his embrace, captured her lips, and made love to her with the voracity of a starving castaway. However the night passed, it was always perfect, their time together a secret paradise.

Madeline worried about his chronic headaches, the cause still a mystery, and whenever she broached the subject of his health, he'd silence her with a hardy kiss. She had learned to let the matter rest — for now. As they approached Caribbean waters, danger lurked behind uncharted islands, through un-navigated currents, and from secluded pirate bays. Soon she would learn the truth about her grandfather.

She held tight the thought of a miracle. She held tight the image of a blessed reunion, of bringing her grandfather home . . . and then a troubling vision always spoiled her joy: a vision of the captain's lone silhouette, standing on the shore of an island as they sailed for England.

Her heart cramped at the unnatural thought of abandoning him in the Bahamas. She'd made several attempts to persuade him to return with them, but he'd doggedly refused, insisting "it was his private affair." For *what* unfathomable reason? she'd cried more than once. But he'd rebuffed her at every turn. He was just determined she keep her part of their bargain and deliver the letter to his sister.

Her soul in turmoil, Madeline rolled across the bed and observed the stubborn, frustrating . . . beautiful man as he studied the sea charts, brow furrowed in complete concentration.

She wasn't his fiancée, much less his wife. He had made no offer of courtship. But the sore matter remained: what would become of them?

Would he ever return to England? Would she ever see him again? And when?

"Am I your mistress?" she queried, voice tart.

He glanced at her from above the slanted desk. "No."

She huffed at the straightforward, passionless answer. "Whore?"

"No!"

His second, more emotional response pleased her better. "Who am I, then?"

"A damn siren I can't get out of my head, my blood, my . . ."

He stopped there. But her heart still surged with delight — and longing. After muttering a few unintelligible words, he returned to the sea charts.

Madeline wasn't finished with him yet, though. "William?"

"Shit." He fisted his palms. "What?"

"I don't want to say goodbye."

He remained fixated on the sea charts, his breathing shallow, loud. When he finally voiced a remark, it was a tattered whisper, "You have to."

In startlingly swift strides, he then left the room, slamming the door behind him.

I'm not angry with you, Maddie.

She had learned long ago his foul moods weren't aimed at her, but something — something potentially devastating — *was* torturing him.

~ * ~

Madeline fingered the letter in her hand. William had given her the paper earlier in the day, sealed with red wax. She had tucked it inside her carpet bag with every intention of delivering the message to his sister, but she now held the parchment with curiosity and agitation.

The captain's neat penmanship addressed the document to "Belle," such an informal greeting, but the letter contained weighty revelations, the same revelations she'd been searching for fruitlessly aboard the *Nemesis*.

Madeline wandered toward the porthole and lifted the paper into the light, but its thickness was too great and she couldn't read the note.

Her fingers trembled with mish-mashed emotions, and at last, she reasoned, she had promised to convey the letter to the duchess, however, she had *not* promised never to read it. She was treading on moral thin ice, she knew, but she was determined to uncover the truth, and since William refused to offer her answers . . .

Before she regained her wits, Madeline pinched the edges of the letter, about to break the wax seal, when William entered her cabin.

He stilled in the doorway, silent, staring at the letter in her hands, then lifted his gaze to her eyes. She waited for him to bellow in outrage, but he remained quiet, unnervingly quiet, and her heart thundered as he stood there, his expression inscrutable.

Madeline clutched the paper, her fingers trembling, her voice trapped in her throat as the moment seemed to stretch endlessly. At last, he moved out of the door frame, walked across the room—and took hold of the letter.

He tugged at it, but she refused to release the paper. Tears filled her eyes. Tears of shame. But he would not look at her again. He finally gripped her hand and forcibly separated her fingers from the letter before he walked out of the room without a single word. Not one rebuke. Not one reprimand. But his silence was louder than any blasted reproof.

She had lost his trust.

Madeline slumped on the bed, her tears falling too fast to soak up with her sleeve . . . so she just let them fall.

That night, she found William on deck. The crew

moved quietly, performing their evening chores. A lookout sat in the nest, spyglass in hand. With the ship secure, the captain had stepped aside and leaned against the rail, stargazing.

She watched him from a distance, almost loathed to break his solitude. She found pleasure in just observing his silhouette. If she shut her eyes, she could trace every contour of his muscular physique, his handsome face with her fingertip.

Quickly she opened her eyes with a heart-squeezing gasp. In truth, she loathed to approach him because she knew their intimacy had been broken — and she might not be welcomed in his arms anymore. Their fellowship might be . . .

She swallowed her misgiving. In slow strides, she approached William as if he were a skittish deer, but she should have remembered he never let anyone get too close, much less sneak up behind him.

"Good evening, Maddie," he said without glancing in her direction.

She settled beside him, unsure of her words. She'd rehearsed an explanation all day, but now, feeling the tension between them, her excuse seemed trite. Aye, her concern for his chronic headaches, his nose bleeds remained, but she had gone about searching for answers in the wrong way.

In the end, she said, "I'm sorry."

The simple truth.

"I believe you," he returned in a calm voice.

A surprise, that. But he'd always had a reasonable temperament — well, most of the time — and she sighed with unbound relief.

"I apologize, too," he said next, his voice

tightening.

She shivered, chilled. "I don't understand."

"I've made a terrible mistake." He finally looked at her, his soul in obvious turmoil. "And I accept full responsibility for it."

Her heart dropped. "What are you saying, William?"

"We had a business arrangement: a straight-forward exchange of services. I would rescue your grandfather, while you would deliver a letter to my sister." He looked off, then. "I broke that bargain when I bedded you, offered you the impression you had a right to interfere in my private affairs. I regret that decision. I am fully to blame for it. I am always in control of my impulses, and I failed to control them these many nights."

"I see."

She didn't see, of course, as her world turned on its ear and muddled her entire soul. She remembered every tender touch and whispered word. She remembered every intimate conversation, every moment of laughter. And it was all a mistake? A failure on his part to maintain control?

She seethed, gripping the rail. "And your demand that I take anything from you, everything from you, if it pleases me?"

"Another mistake."

Her voice turned acrid at his cruel and cutting words. "You make a lot of mistakes, Captain, for a man who proclaims to be in constant control."

His shoulders stiffened at the jibe, but his tone remained unflinching. "It would be wise if we returned to our previous arrangement."

"And what arrangement would that be?"

"The one where I govern this ship . . . and you stay away from me."

As a welter of feeling stormed her breast, she gathered her strength and walked away from him. "Aye, Captain."

CHAPTER 11

William slammed his fist into the cabin wall. Once. Twice. He was such a fool, playing house, pretending death wasn't looming over him, that Madeline wouldn't notice it, ask about it. That she would pretend, too, and ignore the obvious. But it was always there. Death.

He punched the wall again. "Shit!"

He wanted to tear the ship to pieces, to rip up every deck board until the ocean swallowed him. Instead, he braced his hands apart and leaned them against the wall, bowing his head, heaving. He'd have to find the damnable strength to keep away from Maddie until he rescued her grandfather, but even now he burned for her, for the comfort of her touch.

She wasn't to blame for the letter. She wanted the truth. But he wouldn't dare tell her. He wouldn't dare tell anyone. He would give the letter to his lieutenant with orders to pass it to Madeline once the ship reached England. If she read the letter then, it wouldn't matter. His whole family would know the truth by then, and he'd be on the other side of the world. Dead.

Bang. Rattle. Thump.

William listened to the commotion next door. What the devil was Madeline doing? He wanted to throttle the woman. Kiss her. He wanted to toss her overboard. He wanted to take her in his arms and never let her go.

Blast it!

He left his cabin and entered her room, eyed the carnage scattered across the floor: a broken chair, pewter plates, books. Was that the chamber pot broken in half?

She folded her arms under her breasts and lifted her chin in defiance. "It was either the furniture or your head."

Her cheeks were wet, flushed, and his innards twisted at the sight of her pain . . . pain he had caused. He wanted to fix everything that was broken, including her. It was his nature. He had always settled the squabbles between his siblings. He had always cleaned up their social messes, even hauled them away from dangerous spheres, but he had never been immersed in the fray. He was the peacemaker, not the instigator. And now he didn't know what to do to make it right for Madeline.

He shut the door. "Maddie—"

A pewter cup went sailing passed his head, crashed into the wall behind him, then clattered to the floor.

He saw red.

When she reached for a fork, he spanned the room and grabbed her wrist. "I won't tolerate destruction aboard my ship."

That was his prerogative.

"Then you'll have to lock me in the brig, Captain."

And she flicked the fork.

He cocked his head to avoid the utensil before it, too, hit the ground. Her insolence disarmed him. He clinched her other wrist and crossed her arms over her chest, pushing her against the wall.

He spotted the tiny red veins in her green eyes and desired to take back everything he had said to her, but he had said it for her own good—for both their goods.

"Let me go, Maddie."

Her lips trembled. "I know it's easy for a man to dismiss his whore, but I—"

"Damn it, you are *not* my whore!"

"Well, no gentleman would've treated a woman like you treated me unless she *was* his whore."

William sucked a breath between his teeth with such swift force, the air whistled. He dropped his brow, resisting the temptation to kiss away her tears.

"I'm sorry, Maddie."

"I don't forgive you."

But she believed him sincere, the incorrigible woman.

"Stay angry with me, lass," he whispered, his voice strained. "Keep that fire burning in your soul. Hate me, even. It will protect you in the end."

"From what?"

"Trust me, Maddie. I-I cannot give you a future."

It was the closest he had ever come to confessing his secret. He stepped away from her, shaking, sensing he was on perilous ground.

He turned away. "I should go."

"William."

He paused at the door. "What?"

"If you could give me a future, would you?"

At the enduring hope in her voice, he looked over his shoulder. "You are shamelessly persistent, woman."

She huffed, indignant.

"*That*," he clarified, "was a compliment."

And he left the cabin.

~ * ~

Madeline sat in her room, sewing, but she was a wretched seamstress, the repair in the garment a rumpled mess, her finger bandaged from all the times she'd stabbed the tip. She finally tossed the dress aside and curled onto the bed, wrapping her arms around her knees.

For two days she'd fretted, stewed, cried and cursed, but she wasn't any closer to making a decision. Should she let William go? In truth, give up on him? Or should she fight for him like the shamelessly persistent woman he'd claimed to admire? Was he asking her to fight for him in a roundabout way?

She pounded the pillow. The man was impossible. She would never really know what he wanted from her, if anything a'tall . . . so perhaps her choice was easier than she imagined? What did *she* want? To be with William? Or not?

An explosion off the starboard stern shattered her rumination.

Shrieking, she rolled off the bed and onto the floor, covering her head. For several breathless moments, she waited before easing off the ground and peeking through the scuttle. Smoke wafted across the glass. She detected the scent of sulphur. But there were no more canon blasts. No sound of breaking wood. No smell of fire. A warning shot?

She scurried topside, bumping into tars making madcap dashes across the deck. She heard the lieutenant's orders for gun power and manning the canons, shouts to the helmsman to take evasive maneuvers. Amid such organized chaos, she spotted William on the poop, spyglass in hand, as he scrutinized the other ship, fast approaching.

"Her colors, Captain?" hollered the lieutenant. "Spain? Portugal? Or the Jolly Roger?"

"No colors," returned the captain, unflappable.

Madeline's throat closed. Why would a ship attack without revealing its colors? Even pirates raised a flag to signal their intent.

As she sidestepped bustling sailors, she wondered if the attacking ship *was* a pirate rig, the one holding her grandfather hostage, but she quickly dismissed the idea. The *Nemesis* had left port in a hurry, without revealing its destination, so the tropical brigands would never expect Madeline to arrive with a crew of armed privateers to rescue her grandfather. Besides, they were still days away from the Bahamian islands. Who was the other vessel, then? And why was William so calm? Was he always so unnervingly blasé in battle?

"Your orders, Captain?" from the primed lieutenant.

"Stand down."

A silence came over the crew: a funeral-like silence.

Madeline scaled the poop. "What are you doing?!"

"Surrendering," he said with barefaced displeasure.

She snatched the spyglass from him and focused on the other ship, counting its masts and canons. "You're a match for her, William."

"I'm not going to fight her."

"But she'll *sink* us."

"Trust me, Maddie."

"But—"

"Raise the white flag," he roared. "Let her come abreast. Prepare to be boarded, men."

CHAPTER 12

Madeline stood alongside the rest of the crew, watching the unidentified ship lower two skiffs into the sea. Tension aboard the *Nemesis* was as thick as molasses. And there were whispers among the tars about the captain's sanity. She prayed there wouldn't be a mutiny. But she also prayed *for* the captain's sanity. *Trust me, Maddie,* he had said. But she was having a deuced hard time trusting him, the man far too enigmatic.

She glanced over her shoulder. A distance away, William remained atop the poop, his expression impenetrable. He had folded his arms across his chest, defensive, bone-rigid in posture, as his steely gaze observed the advancing rowboats.

Madeline cast her eyes toward the same rowboats, flexing then fisting her palms. What the devil was going on? she wondered. William would never sacrifice his crew and ship. He was a man of war . . . unless there was no war, no danger.

At the peculiar thought, she shot the captain another critical glare, and his uncompromising composure seemed more and more like repressed annoyance. The ship wasn't under threat, she then realized. He was.

As the skiffs reached the hull, William ordered, "Lower the ropes."

But when the uncertain sailors dallied, the loyal lieutenant blasted them for being too slow, and the rope ladders were quickly dropped overboard.

The unfurling rope and wood clattered along the ship's planking before splashing into the water, and then the undeniable sound of climbing boots echoed across the silent ship.

Her heart thundered as the unidentified men ascended the ship's flank, and a primal instinct overcame her — to fight. These men were after William. And William would do anything to protect his ship and crew, even sacrifice himself.

Heads soon appeared above deck.

Madeline braced herself — then gasped.

Captain James Hawkins boarded the ship, his long black hair tied in a queue, his sharp blue eyes as dark and smoldering as gun smoke on a battlefield. He was followed by his exotic wife, Sophia, dressed in breeches and a capable seafarer, it seemed, for she scaled the ship with perfect ease.

Madeline's breast tightened in awe as another, then another brother appeared, their wives in tow, with the Duke and Duchess of Wembury bringing up the rear.

"Maddie!"

Cousin Amy dashed toward her and dragged her into an embrace.

"Are you all right, my dear?"

"I-I'm fine," she stammered, still bewildered. "What are you doing here, Amy?"

Amy glanced warily between the family and William. "There were rumors."

"Rumors?"

She whispered, "Of an abduction."

Madeline groaned. "I assure you, there was *no* abduction. I'm here because . . . It's a long story."

As Amy wrapped a supportive arm around her shoulder, she smiled. "Shall we hear it over a cup of tea?"

Madeline nodded. The strain in the air hadn't lifted, though. There was another reason the family had given chase, she swiftly concluded. It was apparent in their stiff postures. She would have assumed an uncomfortable matter was at hand, but there was also a crisis.

She eyed the Duchess of Wembury, standing at the far end of the ship with her husband, her features ever so resentful, broken even. Edmund looked just as infuriated, Quincy somber, perhaps remorseful. And then there was James, inscrutable, but undoubtedly repressing the same powerful emotions as the rest of his kin.

They had not just come to rescue her from a rumored abduction, she reasoned, even though their grave expressions indicated severe disapproval. There was something more going on between the siblings, something immensely personal.

Madeline had always known William was hiding a dark secret from her, the crew, and likely his family. Was it about to be revealed?

~ * ~

William felt as if he'd been shot in the chest again, his wound gushing unhindered amounts of blood.

He remained unmoving on the poop, watching his entire family descend upon his ship.

The moment he'd recognized his eldest brother's schooner, the *Bonny Meg*, he'd realized his carefully orchestrated plans had been dashed to bits, that fate's unexpected fortune had been a joke—and he would have to confront his tempestuous kin, after all.

His tars greeted Edmund, who'd served aboard the *Nemesis* at one time, as well as Quincy, who was still the ship's official surgeon. The women gathered around Madeline, but his sister, Belle, remained at the other end of the vessel, her eyes digging into him with unforgiving fury.

It was James who finally approached him, his gait slow yet determined. "I want a word with you, brother."

A few minutes later, he and James were alone in the captain's cabin.

"Hullo, sweetheart." James reached into the terrarium and scooped up the snake, coiling her around his forearm. "I've missed you, girl."

William observed their strange exchange from across the room, arms folded. He leaned against the wall and braced the heel of his boot on a chair. "How did you find me?"

"You can't set sail in total secret, not from the Thames," he said, returning the serpent inside the glass enclosure. "When large amounts of food and rum and gun powder are loaded aboard a ship, there's always gossip. And you're a man of habit." He shrugged. "I figured you'd take the same route to the Caribbean as we always did in the past."

At the suggestion he was the predictable brother, the brother who never took any risks, William gritted his teeth. The charge would have pleased him once. Now he was bloody insulted.

"And why am I going to the Caribbean?" he asked in a voice not far from a growl. "You don't really believe I abducted Maddie?"

"Maddie, is it? No, I don't believe you abducted her. I don't know why she's here, in truth. But I know what you're doing." His eyes flared. "Running away."

William kicked the chair across the room with such force, the legs shattered. "Curse Quincy!"

Unperturbed, James persisted, "Don't blame the pup for telling us the truth. *You* should have told us—"

"Told you what?" he stormed. "That I'm sick, like Father? That I'm dying, like Father?" His fist slammed into the wall. "Fuck you, James! You would've done the very same thing. You would never have let us watch you fall apart."

"Damn right. Next time cover your tracks better."

William raked his hair until his scalp pinched. "There isn't going to be a 'next time'."

"Are you sure you're sick . . . like Father?"

"Yes."

"He died seven years ago, Will. Quincy's a member of the Royal College of Physicians now. He can help you."

"What? When did this happen?"

"Quincy received word just before Eddie's wedding. He was going to tell you after the nuptials about his membership, that he wouldn't be serving aboard the *Nemesis* any longer."

"It seems I'm not the only one keeping secrets."

James glowered. "Quincy didn't want to take the attention away from Eddie and Amy on their special day. But you—"

"Enough! I'm glad the pup's settled. I don't have to sack him now. It's my last voyage, after all."

His brother's voice dropped. "Are you sure?"

William paced the cabin, rubbing the back of his stiff neck. "I've already been to the most renowned doctors in London. I've visited the wisest medicine men in Africa. There is *no* cure."

"How much time do you have?"

"Four months, maybe six."

"Were you ever going to tell us?"

"I wrote a letter," he said, then stopped, turned away from his brother. "Maddie was going to deliver it to Belle when she returned to England . . . I want you to leave, James."

"No."

"I don't want any of you with me at the end."

"I understand, but I'm not leaving—we're not leaving."

He fisted his palms. "How can you be such a bloody hypocrite?"

"It's rather easy."

William took in a measured breath, changed his tactic. "I can't believe you brought the women?"

"Did you really think I could leave them behind once they'd heard you were sick?"

"They're in danger, James."

"Why?"

"I'm going to rescue Maddie's grandfather. He's

being held hostage in the Bahamas—by pirates."

"Shit. Quincy didn't mention—"

"Quincy didn't know anything about it. I made the plan with Maddie."

"Maddie again? And why are you doing this for Maddie?"

He next rubbed his aching brow. "She's family."

"She's also a good reason to avoid *us*, maybe even die in battle. You and I are alike, Will."

"Are we?" He confronted his brother again, blood burning in his veins. "I'm the soulless head of this family, while you're its destructive ass. I repair what you've ruined. I clean up what you've razed. And I stand between you and your own insufferable temper. Isn't that what you meant when you said I have no soul, that I can't bleed, that I don't even know love?"

James offered him a queer expression at the uncharacteristic outburst, and William headed for the door before he blubbered any more rot. "Forget it."

But his eldest brother grabbed him by the arm. "It's Maddie, isn't it?"

William jerked his arm away and circled the cabin, his guts twisting, his heart pounding.

"Why?" he gritted. "Why now? Why did I meet her now?"

He released the tension in his bones and turned over the dining table with a wild roar.

"Why now, James? When I'm fucking dying and can't . . . and can't be with her?" His energy spent, William slumped against the wall. "I sometimes wish I had never met her. Other times, I thank the stars I had a short time with her. What am I going to do?"

"Marry her."

"Are you mad? I can't marry her, then leave her a widow."

"She might be pregnant."

William seized. He hadn't even considered . . . *he* hadn't even considered the possibility of a babe. "I never thought about that."

"I guess you're not the soulless head you think you are, that you've got a destructive ass, too."

As his head throbbed, William clutched his temples. "What am I going to do?"

"You have to protect Maddie. She can't come home, pregnant and unwed. I will marry the two of you."

"You?"

"I can marry you aboard my ship. When I record the ceremony in the ship's log, it will be considered a common-law marriage. And if you change your will to include Maddie and any heir she might have, she should be protected."

"What if she refuses to marry me?"

"And ruin her reputation?"

"She doesn't care about her reputation; according to her, she lost it long ago."

"And the babe's reputation? Does she want it labeled a bastard for the rest of its life?"

William thumped his head against the wall. "She doesn't know I'm dying, James."

"I can't help you with that, brother. You'll have to tell her the truth. But first you have to propose to the woman."

CHAPTER 13

"M addie, why didn't you tell me about your grandfather?"

At the wounded note in Amy's voice, Madeline offered a contrite expression. Her cousin had been so gracious, offering friendship to a scandalous woman.

As a child, Amy had been abducted, whisked into the rookeries and presumed dead, but two years ago, she'd returned home. And that's when Madeline had started believing in miracles. She'd penned her cousin a letter of welcome, not expecting a reply because of her tainted past. But Amy had rebuffed all social constraints. She'd responded to the letter with affection, and since then, their old amity had blossomed once more.

As girls, they'd shared a few familial memories. Their grandparents had been siblings, making Amy and Madeline second generation cousins. But as women, they were confidants.

"You had so much to struggle with: the annulment from Gravenhurst, the wedding to Cousin Edmund. I didn't want to impose on your kindness."

"But the risk, Maddie! If anyone other than William had caught you stealing jewels you'd be shipped to the colonies — or hanged!"

"I had to take the risk, Amy. At least, I thought I had to take it. I want to apologize for my behavior on the night of your wedding ball. I should not have pilfered the jewels, placing you and Cousin Edmund in peril. It's just . . . the old man saved my life. He took me in when I was destitute, loved me despite my sins. I . . ."

"I understand, my dear." She set aside her teacup and curled her arms around her cousin. "I know love is a powerful force. It drives us to break every rule and take any gamble, however dangerous."

Madeline admired the young woman's bravery. Amy would always do what was right. She would always follow her heart. And much to Madeline's gratitude and good fortune, Amy's heart had led to their solidarity.

"Maddie, I —" William stilled in the doorway, gathering his features. "Hullo, Amy."

"Hullo, William."

He slipped his hands in his trouser pockets, looking vaguely uncomfortable. "I need a private word with Lady Madeline."

"Yes, of course."

As Amy headed toward the door, he stepped away, allowing her passage, but she paused and wrapped her arms around his waist, pecking his cheek. "It's good to see you again."

She then left the cabin, William's features tightening even more. The captain was quite uncomfortable now.

Madeline furrowed her brow at the strange exchange. "What was that about?"

"It's not important." He shut the door and approached her, his blue eyes as turbulent as rough waters. "You have to marry me."

"I beg your pardon?"

He sighed. "Will you do me the honor of being my wife?"

Madeline jumped from her chair. "I understand the question. I mean, why do you want to marry me?"

"You might be pregnant. It's the honorable thing to do."

His answer, though sensible coming from any other man, riled her.

You're a damn siren I can't get out of my head, my blood, my . . .

What? His heart? His soul? Or something crude, like his prick?

She inhaled an infuriating breath.

When he finished that ambiguous sentence, Madeline would consider his clumsy proposal—and not before.

"No," she said.

"But the babe?"

"What babe? I won't know for several more days, perhaps weeks. And *if* I'm pregnant, we can address the convenience of marriage at that time."

"Convenience?"

She turned away from him, aloof, and collected the tea set.

A growl came up behind her. "There isn't much time, Maddie."

She picked up the silver tray, intent on the galley. "I don't know what you mean."

William blocked the door. "What if I die in battle?"

She gasped—then slammed the tray on the table, the porcelain ringing. "How dare you threaten me!"

"Maddie—"

"You are the seasoned captain of a battle-hardened crew." She stabbed him in the chest with her finger. "Your brother is now here with his ship and support. You will find my grandfather, aim your canons at the pirates' heads, and bring the old man back to me. There isn't going to be a battle. And you are *not* going to die!"

She stormed from the room, her innards twisting with dread. She resisted the thought of William's death. Or that of any other tar. She had come with an armed crew to rescue her grandfather with the full intention of taking the pirates by surprise and avoiding a needless confrontation. And while there was still a risk, a *small* risk of disaster, William had no right to frighten her with that remote prospect just to assuage his bloody honor.

~ * ~

When William returned to his cabin, his siblings were gathered inside the room: James hunched over the sea chart, Edmund reading the ransom note, and Quincy beside the scuttle, gazing outward. His sister poured herself a glass of rum and downed it like a pirate, rather than a duchess.

The nostalgic scene took him back six years, when they'd last served together aboard their father's ship, the *Bonny Meg*. They were all still pirates then, the lot of 'em, but Belle had married the duke soon after, and their lives had dramatically changed course.

James had turned the *Bonny Meg* into a trading rig, William had captained the *Nemesis* as a privateer. Edmund and Quincy had served aboard the *Nemesis* for a time before they'd both discovered other passions: one as a Bow Street Runner, the other a doctor.

And as William stood in the middle of the room, nostalgia quickly withered into something darker: the fact that there would be no more family reunions, that he soon wouldn't see any of them anymore.

William gathered a weighty breath, capping his uncharacteristic emotions. He confessed, "She won't marry me."

"Yes, we heard the shouting next door," said James. "Pregnant or not, she can't take the chance since you're . . ."

"Dying?" supplied William.

The others remained silent.

"You have to marry her," insisted James. "You have to tell her the truth."

"Aye, the truth. I'm sure she'll jump at my proposal when I tell her she's going to be a widow — perhaps saddled with a babe — in a few months."

A rancid bitterness climbed up his throat at the thought of leaving Maddie and possibly his child. He trembled with an uncontrollable pressure in his chest, and he wanted to roar like a trapped bear being bated by a sadistic fate.

"There isn't much furniture left in the room," quipped Edmund, glancing at the broken table and chair, sensing his brother's eminent outburst. "You'll have to pummel the bed."

"Piss off," snapped William.

"The wedding will have to wait," from James. "I have an idea about the pirates."

William clenched his palms. "You are *not* taking on the pirates."

The very thought triggered a dull, pulsing ache in his head. He wasn't dead yet, damn it! And he refused to be cast aside like a bloody invalid. *He* had promised Maddie he'd rescue her grandfather, and he'd every intention of keeping his word!

"No, I'm not," returned James, strangely cool-tempered. "I'll leave that to you, Will." He pointed at the chart. "I will stay a league away with the women aboard my ship. As you approach the sheltered bay, the unexpected sight of your guns and my shadow on the horizon should be enough to force a surrender. Quincy and Eddie will remain on board the *Nemesis* with you; they both know the vessel well after serving aboard her for so many years. If we time the attack just right, in the early morning hours, we won't have to fire a single canon."

His brother's logic was sound, and William offered a brusque nod of approval.

"Are you sure her grandfather is alive?" asked Edmund. "The ransom note is vague and written in a lazy hand."

"Or an illiterate one," offered James. "There's still the matter of the ring that accompanied the letter."

"Dead or alive, Maddie wants her grandfather home." said William, ending the debate.

"Well, then, I bid you goodnight."

Edmund dropped the note on the desk and left the cabin, Belle at his heels. She hadn't said a word during the conversation, nor looked in his direction once, making his gut churn with remorse.

James soon followed her out the door, leaving Quincy and William alone in the room. As the frustrating seconds elapsed, and the treacherous pup still lingered, William snarled, "Get out."

Quincy turned from the scuttle. "I'm sorry, Will."

"Well, I don't forgive you for breaking your word."

"Oh, I'm not sorry about that," he returned, flippant. "The family deserved to know the truth."

His fists balled again. "Then what the hell are you apologizing for?"

"I cursed you, you know?"

William's heart rammed against his chest. "You cursed me? To *die*?"

"What? No! I would never do such a thing."

"Not even after I forced you to marry Holly?"

A short time ago, Quincy had found himself in a compromising situation with a viscount's daughter, and while innocent of the charge of seducing the girl, he'd still refused to follow proper etiquette and marry the woman, saving her reputation. It was then William had intervened, threatened Quincy with banishment if he didn't propose to the lass and set things right.

"I was furious with you at the time, I admit," said Quincy. "It's why I cursed your stone heart, willing a tempestuous wench to one day storm your life and wreck it to bits."

"You're a bloody ass."

"I am apologizing, don't forget."

"Get. Out."

Quincy sauntered toward the door. "I also want to thank you, Will. Holly is the best thing that ever happened to me."

William's heart quivered, then spasmed. As the door shut behind his brother, he heaved a giant breath, strapped for air.

God, what he wouldn't give to have a long life with Maddie. She, too, was the best thing that had ever happened to him, curse or no curse.

CHAPTER 14

Madeline had had enough. She was determined to uncover the truth behind William's peculiar behavior. He seemed dismayed by his family's arrival, yet he loved the lot of them, she knew. He'd threatened to hang her to protect them. Now their presence aboard ship had brought about a startling tension. And why had he proposed to her, nay, demanded they wed, when he'd never even suggested the idea before that day?

A rap at the door; it snapped her from her meditation.

She opened the barrier and lifted a brow. "Captain Hawkins."

"James," he said. "There can only be one captain aboard a ship."

"What can I do for you, James?"

He entered the cabin without waiting for an invitation, his ominous presence filling the small space.

She shut the door behind him. "Do come in."

After prowling the room for a moment, he dropped into a chair. "I have the unenviable task of pleading my brother's case—for your hand in marriage."

She folded her hands across her lap. "I don't see how this concerns you?"

"It concerns you and it concerns my brother, so it concerns me."

She had forgotten the Hawkins family banded together no matter the circumstances, that they looked out for each other's happiness—unlike hers. And just the thought of being part of such a family warmed her to the idea of marriage. Not that she was prepared to accept William's proposal. At least, not until she had some answers . . . and James' unexpected arrival may just be the boon she was looking for.

She joined him at the table. "I will listen to your case."

"I'm not a matchmaker," he groused. "But the affair between you and William must be settled— permanently."

Another threat? He was no better than his brother at proposals. Did all Hawkins men club their women over the heads and drag them to the altars?

But Madeline maintained her temper. She wanted to know the truth about William.

"Our affair is complicated," she said.

"Isn't every affair with a woman?"

He sounded like he spoke from miserable experience.

"William and I have a delicate arrangement."

"An arrangement, eh?"

"He isn't interested in marriage; he's never even broached the matter—until today. Why?"

His blue eyes shifted from one end of the room to

the other. "He realized you might be pregnant."

"Today?"

"Aye, today."

"I find it hard to believe a man of such foresight and planning failed to consider the matter before today."

James growled, "He's not been thinking straight of late."

"Why? His headaches?"

"You know about the headaches? Anything else?"

"What else is there?"

"Blimey." He shot out of the chair, startling her. "I should have sent one of the women to convince you to marry him." And he headed for the door, disgruntled.

"James, tell me!"

He stilled.

She whispered, "Tell me what's happening?"

He sighed, keeping his back to her. "You need to ask William that question."

And he left the room.

As soon as the door closed, Madeline fisted her hands. She circled the cabin for a few restless minutes, stirring up her strength, before she squared her shoulders and stalked toward William's cabin.

The moment she reached the door, her intention to barge into the room withered away. Instead, she quietly opened the door and scanned the space. The broken furniture unnerved her. William's prostrate body in bed disarmed her.

She dropped her shoulders. A part of her didn't want to know the truth anymore, sensing it was painful, perhaps too painful to bear. Another part urged her to learn the truth, however painful, and reconcile with it.

Slowly she approached the bed, her footfalls light. His arm was slumped over his brow. If he was asleep, she didn't want to startle him.

"Hullo, Maddie."

"You heard me?"

"I can smell your perfume."

He slipped his forearm from his brow and gazed at her with a heart wrenching mixture of passion and pain.

She realized, then, she didn't want to hear the truth, after all.

She kneeled beside the bed. "Just tell me one thing."

"What is it?"

"How does the sentence end?"

He looked at her, confused.

She recited, "I am a damn siren you can't get out of your head, your blood, your . . . ? Finish the sentence, William, and I will marry you, however it ends."

He shut his eyes. The muscles in his jaw clenched, squaring his features. At last, he opened his eyes and took an uneven breath.

As he struggled to sit on the edge of the bed, he teetered, and she reached for his arm in support.

After a few more hardy breaths, he cupped her cheeks. "You are a damn siren I can't get out of my head, my blood, my heart. I love you, Maddie."

Her eyes welled with tears. She breathed in the magical words that chased away the guilt, the bitterness, the wretched loneliness in her soul, and smiled, quivering, as brilliant light filled her heart.

"But you wish you didn't love me," she said softly. "I can hear it in your broken voice. I'm not good enough for you, your family because of my past."

"No! I just . . . I just wish I had met you sooner."

His inexplicable response unsettled her, and before she could ask him for an explanation, he resorted to old tactics and kissed her soundly, silencing her.

"Will you marry me?" he whispered.

"Aye," she said, breathless.

CHAPTER 15

The next morning, the family gathered aboard the *Bonny Meg* for the wedding ceremony. The decks were scrubbed clean, the sails billowing. The Union Jack had been hoisted now that they were in British waters.

Madeline had borrowed a pink lace and chiffon dress from Cousin Amy for the occasion. Its flowing hemline was just right for a sultry, outdoor wedding. Her hair was braided and pined in swirls, garnished with lavender, which was carried on board for medicinal purposes. And her bouquet consisted of other fragrant herbs from the galley, tied with ribbon.

Madeline soon stood across from William, adorned in dark breeches and polished boots. His shirt was crisp white, his black vest pressed, and a short red scarf was knotted around his neck. The wind teased his ebony locks, and she considered him the most handsome man she had ever seen. His gaze connected with hers, and their eyes never wavered from one another.

As James stood between them, reciting a few lines about matrimony, she scarcely heard the vows . . . or the lapping waves against the ship's hull and the creaking deck boards, the taut ropes groaning under pressure and the sails swelling beneath gusts of air. The marine noises sounded like distant whispers. There was only the heavy drumbeat of her heart pounding in her ears, and a fluttering sensation in her belly that distracted her from her surroundings.

At some point, she heard the words "man and wife" and heaved a desperate breath, as if her head had been below water up until that time. The instant they were wed, a resounding cheer spread across the ship and rice peppered the air.

Madeline's blood surged ever harder as her husband — *her* husband — stepped toward her and pinned her flushed cheeks between his palms, bussing her lips with a sweet, soft kiss.

"Hurrah!" from the crew and family again.

And she smiled, the moment perfect.

Dancing, drinking and food soon followed and lasted into the night. Many of the sailors were talented musicians and lutes and fiddles filled the starry sky with festive folks tunes. Feet stomped in reels and salted fish roasted over iron stoves, making the nautical reception as brilliant as any ball in London.

Of course, the ribald taunts started soon enough, crude smooching noises and teasing remarks about the wedding night from the drunken crew — and her new brothers-in-law.

Madeline had just finished a jig with Cousin Edmund, breathless, when the innuendos heated her already rosy cheeks. She glanced at William, leaning against the main mast, a tin mug in his hand. He watched her with such an intensity in his eyes, her lungs gasped for air.

After several more moments of silent observation, he sauntered toward her and the cacophony of bawdy voices increased. As he extended his hand, she blushed down to her toes. "Let's get away from this ruckus," he said in a smoky voice, his eyes just as smoldering.

She took his offered hand, so hot. He clamped hers in a protective, unmistakably possessive hold, and she shuddered at the newfound intimacy between a husband and wife.

William escorted her to a cabin that had been especially prepared for them, alight with lamps and dressed with fresh bedding. At the washstand, a bowl of steaming water, oil and herbs infused the room with the aroma of a wild garden.

Madeline heard the latch shut behind her, and her heart pounced with anticipation.

"You look lovely," he murmured.

"Thank you."

Her skin prickled with gooseflesh, and she twisted her fingers in an absentminded fashion. She had spent many nights in William's arms, his bed. Why was the thought of being with him now so very different?

"I need help with the buttons at the back of my dress."

His heavy footfalls approached her—and stilled. She heard his labored breathing, sensed his robust strength. He was inches away from her, but it was still too far. She wanted him even closer, deeper.

At last he touched her. She tightened under the

tender brush of his knuckle at the nape of her neck before he grazed the curvature of her spine, right down to the small of her back.

The long, slow, and blatantly sensual, stroke ignited her blood, and she quivered with longing. But after the sensuous touch, he moved away from her, stopping beside the scuttle.

Her throat dry with want, she asked, hoarse, "What's the matter?"

He folded his arms across his chest, his eyes covered by shadows. "I don't think we should have a wedding night, Maddie."

"Why? Do you have headache?"

He shook his head in denial.

If he wasn't ill, then . . . "You don't want to be with me anymore?"

He had performed his duty. He had married her, securing her reputation and that of any babe, but now he rebuffed their marital relationship: a relationship he'd never wanted until his brothers had forced him to do the honorable thing.

"I want to be with you," he rasped with vehemence. "Always."

And she sighed with indescribable relief. "What's wrong, then?"

He pulled a letter from his trouser pocket, stared at it for a moment before he said, "This is the note I wrote to my sister: the one I asked you to deliver upon your return to England." He handed her the sealed message. "I'd like you to read it."

Madeline took the familiar paper, her fingers trembling. She also took in a fortifying breath. She knew, intuitively, the letter was going to change her life forever.

Tears filled her eyes even before she broke the wax seal, and anger replaced the want in her bones. He would deny her the pleasure of a wedding night, she thought with bitterness. Her first night in his arms as his wife would be dashed by the devastating news in the letter. And she knew the news was devastating. She felt the weight of the words in her hand; it pressed on her palm, her arm, her body until she dropped in a chair, unable to stand.

~ * ~

A welter of feeling raged in William's breast as he watched his wife collapse in a chair, holding the letter in her quivering hand. He wanted to snatch the blasted note from her and tear it into pieces, to make love to her one last time . . . but if she wasn't pregnant, it was better she remained that way. He wouldn't take her to bed, knowing he'd leave her a widow with a child.

A selfish part of him didn't give a damn about the future; he cursed it to hell. He had always done what was right, what was honorable, what was expected of him: the reasonable, levelheaded brother. And for once, he yearned to break the bars of his suffocating prison . . . but he couldn't break anything without also breaking Maddie's heart. And that hurt worse than any bullet in the chest.

She deserved to know his fate. As his wife, it was her fate, too.

Madeline opened the seal and unfurled the paper. Her eyes glazed over his penmanship, her features inscrutable.

His lungs seized as he waited for her response,

and as the insufferable silence stretched, he wavered between addressing her and holding her . . . but soon the letter flittered from her fingers and gently touched the ground.

Without looking in his direction, she stood up and headed for the door, the heel of her shoe crushing the paper as she hastily retreated, rejecting him.

William girded his muscles, holding back a torrent of inexplicable, overwhelming emotion. *It's better this way*, he told himself. It was better she hated him, so when he was gone, she wouldn't mourn him. She wouldn't feel any hurt. Yet still . . .

It was several minutes before he could breathe at a normal pace. Why was he feeling so damn much now? At the end of his life?

The moment he had the strength to walk, he thundered from the cabin, topside.

Amid the revelry, he searched for James. The second he spotted his eldest brother, he grabbed him by the arm and hauled him toward the edge of the ship.

"What the devil are you doing here?" demanded James. "If your wedding night is over already, I'll be mighty . . ." The banter ended there. After a thoughtful pause, "You told her the truth, didn't you?"

"I did," he gritted.

James looked over his shoulder, searching for the bride, no doubt, but she wasn't to be found on deck. "I'm sorry, Will."

"I'm going back to my ship. I need a boat."

"And Maddie?"

"She's staying aboard with you. I'll send over her

belongings in the morning."

"I'll fetch Eddie and Quincy."

"Why?"

"They're going back to the *Nemesis* with you."

He growled, "I don't need nursemaids."

"But you need a boat."

In other words, 'take the fledglings or swim back to the *Nemesis*.' Though tempted to jump ship as suggested, William gritted, "Fine."

James left to make the arrangements.

William inhaled the salty air and shut his eyes, still fighting to keep the anguish in his breast from bursting through his ribs. When a feminine hand brushed his lower back and a head propped on his shoulder, he sighed.

"I'm still angry with you, you know?"

William opened his eyes and kissed the top of his sister's golden head. She mirrored their mother with her blonde locks and umber eyes, while the rest of them resembled their father: black tresses and sea blue eyes.

"I'm sorry, Belle."

She sniffed and parted from him. "Is everything all right between you and Maddie?"

"No."

"I'm sorry to hear that." She removed a thin chain from her neck, a gold ring at the end. She held the chain straight until the bauble tumbled into her hand. "I want you to have this, Will."

He recognized the ring. It had belonged to their father. "But he gave it to you for your twentieth year." She cherished the ring. Wore it always.

"And I'm giving it to you on your wedding day.

For luck."

He accepted the gift with uneasy gratitude, fingering the bauble: a man's ring with a winged hourglass for an emblem, a pirate's ring warning time was getting away. "Thank you."

"You're welcome."

She walked away then.

William curled his palm around the ring, *feeling* time flying away . . . but there was nothing he could do to stop it, much less turn it around.

CHAPTER 16

William entered his cabin and slammed the door behind him. He'd come aboard the *Nemesis* with Quincy, Edmund and a few of his tars who'd been present at the wedding. The other sailors had remained onboard to guard the ship and keep it on course.

William now regretted inviting even a few of his men, for they'd witnessed his return to ship without his wife. He'd made it clear to them she was staying aboard the *Bonny Meg* with the rest of the women for reasons of safety, as they were about to embark on the raid of the pirate camp, and while the excuse was wholly sound, he couldn't explain the early departure from the *Bonny Meg*—before the wedding night was over. He had remained silent on that matter, and the wise sailors knew not to make any remarks.

The moment William was inside the privacy of his quarters, he thrashed what was left of the table and chair, reducing the furniture to splinters.

His energy spent, he dropped on the edge of the bed and stared at the ring on his middle finger, his father's ring. He could suddenly hear the sands of time passing through the hourglass of his life, and the noise grated on his ears.

He had never been so aware of his mortality, not even in the heat of battle or when he'd struggled to survive after being shot. He was more aware of it than ever before because of Maddie, because of the time he wouldn't have to be with her—or their child. If she was pregnant, the babe would grow up without any memory of him, without any essence he'd had a father.

William knew his brothers would step in and help raise the boy into a man. If a daughter was born, there would be plenty of uncles to protect her from harm, like fortunes hunters.

But he fisted his hands at the thought of others doing his duty, and not just because it *was* his duty, but because he wanted to be there for his family.

William suddenly wondered why his sister had given him the ring: to torture him? He knew she still resented him for leaving England without revealing the truth about his illness, for wanting to perish off shore without saying a proper farewell.

He tugged on the ring, but the damned thing was wedged firmly on his finger. He twisted and yanked it without success, then finally realized there was only one way to remove it: chop off his finger.

A pert voice then suggested, "Try butter."

William glared at the impudent tar with his scruffy knee breeches and wrinkled shirt. A cap concealed his tousled hair, the brim low, covering his eyes.

For a moment, William was stunned by the boy's audacity at entering the captain's cabin without knocking, much less waiting for an invitation, but he quickly replaced his confusion with rage and bounded to feet, prepared to toss the boy into the brig for his insolence.

But before William scruffed him, the lad removed his cap and long ginger locks tumbled over his—her—shoulders.

Maddie.

He staggered backward. She looked like an urchin. What was she doing in his room? How had she come aboard ship?"

As the flurry of thoughts distracted him, she closed the space between them—and slapped him.

"That was for taking so long to tell me the truth." She smacked his other cheek. "And that was for ruining my wedding night."

After she'd released her upset, she kicked about the pieces of broken furniture. "Why didn't you tell me sooner, William?"

"I never intended to marry you."

"What?"

"When I first met you," he clarified. "I intended to rescue your grandfather and send you both home to England with the letter to my sister."

"The letter mentioned your father's illness."

A stiff nod.

"And you're sick? Like him?"

"Aye."

"I see." She then crossed her arms over her chest and glared at him. "Well?"

His cheeks still smarting, his ears still ringing, he wondered, bemused, "Well what?"

"What are you going to do to make it up to me?"

"Maddie—"

"I'll tell you what you're going to do." She huffed. "First, I want my wedding night—and it'd better be an attentive one. Second, I want a child. In that order," she emphasized.

He was still too dazed to breathe, much less respond.

"How?" he finally rasped. "How did you get on board the *Nemesis*?"

"Do you like the disguise?" She stretched the breeches at the hips, much too large for her figure and tied with rope. "Quincy and Eddie helped me fashion it, then bundled me into the row boat."

"Why the hell would they do that?"

Had his younger brothers accosted her? Forced her aboard his ship, trying to make things right between the newlyweds? It was just the sort of asinine—

"Because I asked them to," she quipped.

His breath hitched. "What?"

"Your sister was kind enough to pin my hair beneath the cap. She's rather good at making a woman look like a man."

"They all know?"

"That I came aboard the *Nemesis*? Aye, so don't fret. No one thinks I'm missing, that I had an accident and fell overboard."

"Why?" was his next query; the hardest question he'd ever asked her. After dropping the letter on the ground and grinding it with her heel, she had made her sentiments toward him clear—she loathed him.

"Because I want to be with you," she said softly.

"Then why stow away? Why not just come to

me?"

"I knew you were angry with me."

"No." He shook his head, resisting the temptation to believe her. "You left the room without a look or a word. *You* left."

"I was overwhelmed."

"You stomped on the letter."

"I wasn't watching my step. I just wanted to run away from the truth. But I couldn't run away from it... I love you, William."

He had never heard those words from a woman not his kin. He had never opened his heart to any woman, and if he was honest, not even Maddie, for she'd reached into his chest and stolen his heart. He couldn't breathe after her declaration.

She nestled against him, pressing her body into his, molding herself to him — and setting his blood on fire.

"I want to be with you, however much time remains. And I want a child — your child." Her voice cracked. "If you can't be with me forever, I want a part of you with me always."

William remained stone hard, resisting the reckless proposal, then he remembered his father's ring and its meaning: time getting away. And he realized his sister hadn't given him the ring to torment him, but to remind him time was precious. He should spend it wisely. He should spend it in love.

A peace settled over him, and he curled his fingers around the back of his wife's neck, pulling her in for a tender kiss.

He tasted the briny tears on her lips, and his

primal instincts were aroused: to protect her, to take away her pain, and to make her happy.

CHAPTER 17

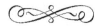

The moment her husband bussed her lips, the world righted itself. How strange that a single kiss had the power to raise broken dreams, heal wounds, and chase away dark shadows. One. Pure. Kiss.

Another miracle, Madeline thought, as he drew her deeper into his embrace, threading his fingers through her mussed hair, caressing her mouth with slow and deliberate thrusts. So attentive.

She relished the sensuous feel of him. Her blood warmed, then simmered. Her skin prickled, then shivered.

A steamy hand soon dipped under her shirt and played across the knobs of her spine, feathery strokes, so teasing, yet so full of sensual intent. She shuddered, over and over. Her heart hastened. She clinched his arms, holding him tight, then tighter still . . . like a storm brewing in the distance.

"Lift your arms," he bade, his hot lips still brushing hers.

Her lungs quickened. She eased her grip on his arms. Gently, he hoisted the shirt over her head. Her hair rained across her backside. Her breasts swelled

ALEXANDRA BENEDICT

in the heady night air. Her nipples puckered, lengthened with want.

Another buss, more firm, stirred a soft moan from her throat. His strong hands went to her hips, unfastened the rope at her waist. The trousers dropped to the floor with ease, and she kicked them aside. Naked. Throbbing. Waiting.

He removed his own shirt and vest, more hastily than he'd tended to hers. He almost ripped the red scarf from his neck. But when he reached for his trousers, she stopped him, enveloped his hands and set them aside, fingering the buttons herself . . .

As she tugged and pulled, unhooking one button, then another, she sensed the man's taut muscles vibrating, every titillating hum, and it stoked her own desire even more.

He growled at her slow progress. "You must really be pissed at me."

She smiled inward.

"It's my wedding night," she whispered, nipping his chin with her teeth. "I intend to enjoy every moment of it—so keep still."

His muscles hardened.

"Better," she murmured.

As she loosened the final button, parting the flap, she gathered her breath, quivering, and slipped her hand across his hard length.

"Maddie!" he cried and dropped his head back in ecstasy. Or perhaps surprise. Or both. But the way he shouted her name, as if it were torn from his throat, thrilled her.

She raked her bottom lip with her teeth, dazed by her own bold gesture. She cusped his erection, tracing the thick veins of his cock, rubbing him with a primal impulse that defied all her good breeding— and good sense. Tempting a man like William would get her a rough bedding, not a tender one. But she clasped him just the same. And her control over him was more tasty than breath.

She pressed her breasts, so aroused, into his chest, and ordered, "Take off your pants."

His eyes lighted on her again, almost black with lust, and her heart spasmed. He stripped off his trousers and together, bare fleshed, they stood in each other's presence for a tense moment . . . before he steered her toward the bed.

Her nerves thrummed in expectation as they tumbled onto the mattress. He covered her with his hot body, captured her mouth in a ravenous kiss, and wrapped a muscular arm around her waist. She tasted the salty spray of the sea on his skin, felt his muscles jump and caper under her explorative touch. She hungered for him. So deep in her soul.

He rolled her on her side in a swift movement, and she offered a startled gasp. Her unruly hair whirled and landed across his face, where he buried his lips against the back of her throat.

"William!"

He ignored her entreaty, wedged his leg between her moist thighs. Her heart thundered at the uncompromising position he'd placed her in, her back caged against his chest. But when his wicked hand grazed the length of her torso, slipping between her flushed breasts, across her taut midriff, and over her pulsing clit, she seized in pleasure.

"William," she groaned in surrender this time.

She thought she heard a grunt of satisfaction, but her thoughts soon disbanded as he lifted her thigh higher, opened her quim wider—and pushed inside her with a hard thrust, stretching her, making her arch in a maelstrom of unfamiliar sensations. She squeezed her muscles, but his raspy voice tickled her ear with, "Trust me, Maddie."

At his comforting words, she eased her flexed tendons and joints and settled against him. He rocked her. So slow at first. It took her several moments to respond to his rhythm and match his tempo, but soon she undulated in blissful harmony with him, unleashing soft whimpers as he pounded her core with ever deeper, ever quicker penetrations.

"Yes," she cried. "Yes!"

She gasped with every rutting stroke, her quim trembling, so wet with need. The tense pressure building at her clit released, and she let out a passionate scream. Her muscles throbbed. Fluids streaked her thighs, draining her of strength.

William rammed her hard, seeking his own orgasm, bumping her hips in frantic strokes before he spasmed inside her with a feral groan.

The couple stilled.

Madeline gathered her pulse and steadied her heartbeat, offering a euphoric sigh, and a little voice inside her told her he'd given her everything that she'd wanted—even a child.

She smiled in a dreamy fashion. "A good bedding is very troublesome. It takes so much effort."

The husky chuckle at her backside quickly evolved into hearty laughter. "Hell, woman. Was that a complaint?"

"A compliment," she assured him, still catching her breath.

He rolled her again, bringing her flush with his handsome features. He pushed aside her tousled hair and bussed her lips. "I love you, Wife."

Her heart fluttered. "And I you, Husband."

His lashes flickered. She sensed his drowsiness. But she wasn't about to let their wedding night end so soon.

She nudged his nose, grazed his cheek with her fingertips. "Tell me about your past, William?"

"Now?"

"Yes, now. I want to know everything about my husband."

It might have been wiser to learn more about the man before she'd married him, but most newlyweds knew even less about one another, their courtships public or supervised by chaperones.

"There isn't much to tell," he hedged.

"Your sister married a duke. You sailed the seven seas for twenty-five years. And there isn't much to tell?"

In truth, she wanted to hear about his life. She wanted to know every detail about the man, to treasure his tales and, one day, to pass them on to their child.

He smoothed the frown lines from her brow with the pad of his thumb. "Fine."

At his warm caress, she balled up the pillow, resisting the swell of emotion in her breast, and listened.

"Once upon a time—"

"Stop." she sighed. "What are you doing?"

"I'm telling you a fairy story." He tucked his muscular arm under the pillow. "My sister married a duke, after all."

"I'd like an honest tale."

"No embellishments?"

"If you please, luv."

He offered her a smoldering look at the sassy endearment, and it warmed her unlike any blanket or fire. She savored the warmth and waited. And waited.

Her husband wasn't much of a conversationalist, it seemed. A good listener, aye, but otherwise not one for chitchat, so she prodded, "How was your boyhood?"

"Fine."

She rolled her eyes.

"James and I were content," he said at last. "Our father, Drake, worked as a carpenter. He made a good income and we wanted for naught. Our mother, Megan, dotted on us. We were lucky . . . for a time."

"What happened?"

"One night, Father didn't come home. Twelve years passed before we saw him again."

She gasped. Twelve years! "Where had he been all that time?"

He seemed perturbed, and she offered him a moment to reflect, to regain his composure before he resumed with:

"He'd been abducted by a press gang and forced to serve aboard a naval vessel."

Madeline fisted her palm and brought it to her lips. She had heard about such injustice during the eighteenth century, when The Royal Navy was desperate for sailors. Few enlisted voluntarily because of poor pay and even poorer treatment, so press gangs were hired to kidnap young and healthy men and drag them aboard ships.

"For ten years," said William, "Father remained imprisoned, malnourished and mistreated."

"And the last two years?" she whispered.

"The naval vessel was attacked by pirates, raided for supplies. But before the pirates returned to their own rig, their captain, Dawson, offered the weary sailors an opportunity to join his crew—and Father accepted. He turned traitor."

"I understand." After a decade at sea, away from his family, abused . . . it was enough hardship to turn any man traitor. "So your father was a pirate for two years?"

"Aye. He and Dawson became friends. My father was quick with a mallet and nail, repaired the ship after every battle. It earned him a place in Dawson's good book. The pirate captain even gave my father this ring."

Madeline eyed the large band around her husband's finger, the emblem an hourglass with wings. Strange, she thought. She'd never noticed the ring before tonight. "What does the symbol mean?"

"Time getting away. It appeared on some pirate flags at the time, hoisted just before an attact, warning the other ship her luck was running out."

"I've never seen you wear the ring."

He twisted the band around his finger. "It belonged to Belle. It was a gift from our father for her twentieth year. A reminder not to flitter away time. It's too precious." He paused, then, "Belle gave it to me tonight, as a wedding gift."

He seemed moved by the gesture from his sister, but the ring—or rather its message—unnerved Madeline.

"What happened, then?" she asked, shaking off the unsettling sensation. "Between your father and Dawson?"

"After two years touring the Caribbean, Father had paid his debt to Dawson. He asked to be released, to return to his family in England. Dawson didn't want to lose my father's carpentry skills, but he agreed—reluctantly—on the ground of their friendship. He let my father go with his fair share of the stolen bounty.

"The years had been hard for us without Father. James and I assumed him dead. But Mother never lost hope he'd come home. And one day, he did. Belle and the others came along soon after, until Mother died in childbirth to Quincy."

"I'm sorry, William."

He rubbed his brow. "James and I reared the babes, while Father took to the sea as captain of his own ship, the *Bonny Meg*, named after our mother. We later joined him. A governess was hired to look after the fledglings, until they, too, came of age."

"So you travelled the world with your father, trading at exotic sea ports, meeting exotic peoples. You and Grandfather have so much in common."

"Exotic sea ports, aye, but we didn't travel as merchants."

"Oh?"

He stopped there.

"Go on, William. Were you privateers? Explorers, like Grandfather?"

"Pirates."

As the word seeped into her pores, her blood simmered, and she scrunched the pillow harder and harder. "P-pirates?" She almost choked on the word. "You're a pirate?"

"Retired."

As if that made a bleedin' difference. She thumped his shoulder, then pounded it, then slapped him so hard, her fingers ached. "You hypocrite!" She crawled away from him, kneeling on the bed. "You threatened to hang *me* for theft, called *me* a pirate when we first met, and *you're* the rotten buccaneer?!"

"Retired," he repeated.

She slapped him again. "How dare you! I can still feel the threat of the noose around my neck?"

He blocked her blows. "Maddie, I was protecting Edmund and Amy at the time."

"I know," she hollered, her heart hammering. "You're still a wretched hypocrite!" She dropped on the bad and turned her back toward him, heaving.

"Maddie . . ."

"I'm tired. Goodnight."

A second later she shrieked as he pulled her into his arms, smothered her in an intimate embrace. "You will not go to sleep angry with me, woman."

"And what do you intend to do about it?"

At first, he made no movement . . . but then his treacherous fingers caressed her arm in sensual strokes, and his hypocritical lips bussed her throat, and his manipulative tongue slipped into her mouth, stirring every nerve and muscle to sensuous arousal.

She nipped his tongue.

"Bloody hell, woman!"

"I'm still mad," she huffed. "Do not seduce me, *pirate*."

He sighed, licking the blood from his lips. "Maddie, it's been six years since I was a pirate. As soon as Belle married the duke, we *all* retired from piracy, to protect her. When I met you, I didn't want my past catching up with me. Or my family."

She could accept that—though she was still furious.

"Pirate," she mumbled, still in disbelief. "I married a bloody pirate."

CHAPTER 18

His arm around his wife's shoulder, his cheek pressed over her brow, William slumbered in easy rest—until heaven split apart and hell rained down on the ship.

At first, he thought the slashes of light and shuddering deck boards a night terror, but when the rig lurched at a sharp angle, the violent pitch sent him tumbling out of bed and slamming into the ground.

His every bone ached under the thrashing, his eyes captured lights of ethereal beauty before the bow crashed back into the sea, tossing him against the other side of the cabin.

Jesus!

His features grimacing, he gathered his strength and balance and searched for Madeline. He spotted her clinging to the bedpost, the bed sheets coiled around her body like a snake.

"William!"

As the rig rolled again, they both lobbed at its mercy, but the sound of his wife's desperate scream for help filled him with unbound energy, and he snatched a leather belt skittering across the floor.

Thunder drummed. Wood splintered.

William ignored the cataclysmic sounds as he plowed toward Madeline. He lashed the belt around her waist and secured her to the bedpost. After a hard, reassuring kiss, he ordered, "Stay here!" And prayed the woman obeyed him just *once*.

Amid heavy swells, William managed to pull on his trousers and head topside. He stumbled into walls and staggered under reeling surges before reaching the hatch and scaling the ladder into the swirling squall.

For a moment, his heart stopped pumping as he gawked at the billowing black clouds funneling water into the sky. A ravenous comber rammed him, then. The foamy wave swiped everything not fastened to the ship, and William grabbed hold of a rope before being sucked into the churning waters.

Had the world turned upside down?

The ship listed dangerously to one side. A glance toward the unmanned helm shot a chill down his spine—the ship was adrift.

He wrapped his wrists around the ropes lashing in the gale, making his way toward the helm, hunkering every time another hungry breaker beat the decking, taking his breath away.

When he finally reached the helm, he latched onto the ship's wheel. The pressure from the monstrous storm had him grinding his teeth as he shifted all his weight to the wheel, keeping the vessel afloat.

Under streaks of lightening, William spotted figures reefing the sails. Another flash illuminated the *Bonny Meg* on the distant horizon. But the next blue blaze of electric light silhouetted a mountaintop.

An island.

"Hard to starboard!" he shouted, warning the crew as he rotated the wheel to avoid landfall, but it was far too late for the evasive maneuver. His draft too low, the water too shallow, the rig ran aground with a tremendous lurch and groan.

William hit the deck. Hard. The dark sky descended on him. He heard the hull breaking apart on the rocks and thought of Maddie, his heart splintering like the ship, before he blacked out . . .

~ * ~

When William opened his swollen eyes, the soft glow of dawn invaded his vision. It took him several more moments to adjust to the dusty pink light and focus on the debris scattered across the beach.

What the hell had happened?

He moaned under the weight of planking across his chest, and with a tortured breath, tossed the jagged wood aside. As the gentle tide caressed his bare feet, the sensation roused him from his muddled mindset. He was half buried in the sand and rolled to one side, his features twisting in agony.

A snake slithered passed him: a yellow boa.

His head soon crowded with memories. A ship. A storm. A wife.

"Maddie," he rasped, his throat burning with salt water. "Maddie!"

The coast was littered with wreckage, bruised and battered tars. He sighted Edmund and Quincy on their uneven feet, assisting the injured seamen. The *Bonny Meg* wasn't on the horizon anymore. Had she drifted to the other side of the island? And Maddie. Where was Maddie?

He scanned the tropical shoreline, but there was no sign of his wife.

God, no!

He struggled upright . . . and his heart dropped at the sight of the *Nemesis*, her hull cracked in two. Her stern was low in the water, her bow pitched on a peninsula of boulders. Her masts had collapsed under the force of the impact, her sails draped over the decking like burial shrouds.

Conviction replaced confusion. He trudged through the wet sand and surf, cutting the soles of his feet on sharp rock, ignoring the stinging pain as he waded toward the shattered ship in desperate strides.

He reached the massive crevice and climbed inside the hulk, water up to his waist, and plodded through the passageways, making his way up the decks. As he neared his cabin door, he noticed it was shut. His heart pounded in his chest like a steam engine, the pressure building as he reached for the latch.

Jammed.

He slammed his shoulder into the door, breaking it down.

"Maddie!"

But Maddie was gone.

A tear in the hull's siding let in the morning light: a tear wide enough for a woman to fall through— and be swept out to sea.

He staggered toward the hole and latched on to the rough siding. There, floating in the water, was a belt: the very belt he'd used to secure his wife to the bedpost.

His heart stopped.

Hope died.

As blood rushed into his brain, William collapsed on his knees. He girded every muscle, suppressing the swirling grief in his soul from spilling out, but there was nowhere for the insufferable pain to hide, and at last, he howled like a wild animal trapped in a snare.

His chest cramped until air was scare, making his vision blur. As he gazed, listless, out to sea, he spotted a trail of debris up the coast. He inhaled a much-needed breath and observed the distant shoreline, his foggy mind swelling with a distinct memory.

He whispered, "She can swim."

Her grandfather had taught her to swim as a child, a skill most sailors didn't even possess. Could she have washed further ashore? Could she have survived?

His heart beat with renewed hope. She had survived scandal and banishment. The death of her first love. The possible death of her grandfather. She. Had. Survived.

And she had survived the wreck, he was sure.

William slogged through the tangled ship. Once on the beach, Quincy approached him, his face bruised, a cut under his eye.

"Six men missing, Captain, including the first lieutenant."

William nodded. "Take the rest of the men into the bush. Treat the wounded as best you can. And wait for help." A dagger in the sand captured his attention. He swiped the weapon. "Eddie!"

His middle brother approached. "Aye?"

"You've been promoted to first lieutenant. Let's find our missing men. And my wife."

CHAPTER 19

Madeline released the driftwood and crawled ashore, spitting up seawater. Her lungs burned. Her chest cramped. She crumpled onto the sandy beach, gasping for air. Disoriented. Bemused. Weak.

She hardly remembered what had happened, her mind a whirl of deafening thunder and lightning that sizzled and streaked the sky. She had been tied to the bedpost, she thought. William had kissed her. And then the walls had come apart, and a tremendous force had broken the bed. After that, water. Unbound water.

The surf brought in bits of wood and rope, pots and mugs. She spotted a white garment and scooped it from the receding tide, wringing the fabric for she was as naked as Eve before The Fall.

Grimacing, she wriggled into the linen chemise. At least one of her ribs were broken, if not more, and she scoured the bank, seeking the crew, her husband . . . but she was alone on the coast.

Was she the sole survivor of the wreck?

A sob welled in her throat. She choked on her tears. What about the *Bonny Meg*? If still afloat, she would have rescued the men of the *Nemesis*.

Madeline cradled her battered side as she searched the horizon for the *Bonny Meg*, but there was no sign of the other schooner. She needed to find the *Nemesis*. She needed to know if the others had lived. She needed help. And hope.

Struggling to gain her footing, she stumbled and plopped on her bottom. The storm had flogged her mercilessly. She felt numb. Parched. But she couldn't stay on the beach. As the sun climbed, the temperature also mounted. She needed shelter or the rising heat and humidity would ravage her.

She cast her bleary eyes toward the tree line, about a hundred feet away. And as she dragged her body across the coarse sand, she cried out with each awkward movement. But she had to reach the shade of the palms. She had to find water. And she had to hide.

What if there were pirates on the island? The very ones holding her grandfather for ransom? She still had to rescue the old man.

Leaves rustled.

Madeline stilled.

Slowly she lifted her head, eyeing the greenery — and noticed the ferns fluttering. "Is anyone there?"

A colonist? An animal? A seaman?

Or a pirate?

She winced as she propped her upper body on her elbows. "Hullo?" she croaked.

The ferns flickered again and gangly fingers spread apart the foliage, revealing a scrawny lad of about twelve hunkering in the sand. He stared at her with a wide-eyed expression, scruffy, his skin smudged with dirt, but Madeline trusted him despite his bedraggled appearance. She sensed he had a kind heart.

"I need help," she said, stirring into a sitting position. She huffed, exhausted. "I can't walk."

The boy craned his neck, observing one end of the coast then the other.

"There is no one else here," she assured him, swallowing the lump in her throat. "I'm alone."

He looked at her again, agog, before he scampered from the bushes and dashed toward her.

The lad crouched beside her. His lanky arm went around her waist. She curled her own arm over his shoulder, and with surprising ease, he hoisted her to her feet.

Together they tottered into the woods. The air cooler, Madeline sighed. She grabbed a palm for support and eased her aching limbs across its sagging trunk.

"Thank you," she rasped.

As her bones throbbed, she gritted her teeth, holding her broken ribs. The boy watched her, alarmed, then sprinted off.

"Wait!" she cried.

But the thicket closed around him. Damn. Why had he left her?

Or had he?

The sound of crinkling foliage under furious feet prickled her ears. Branches snapped. Vines shimmied. And the boy returned. He handed her a leaf, coiled into a makeshift cup and filled with water. She almost cried at the offering.

"Bless you."

She captured the leaf and downed the cold, fresh water, and even as it roiled in her gullet, diluting the sand and salt, it was still the most wonderful thing she had ever tasted.

Soon her strength improved in the shade. Her gaze fell back on the boy. He had stepped a few yards away, crouching in the shrubbery.

"Do you have a name?"

His cheeks flushed. Perhaps he was a wild child, she thought with dismay. An orphan? Had he survived in the jungle alone? She had heard of such cases. But there was intelligence in the boy's wide eyes. If he was mute, he wasn't dumb.

"I'm Maddie."

He nodded, smiling.

"Yes, Maddie. It's my name. You do understand, don't you?"

He nodded again.

At least she could communicate with him—somewhat. "Do you know the island?"

Another bob of the head.

"A ship ran aground this morning." She opened her arms, emphasizing, "A big boat. I need to find it."

The youngster screwed up his face, wary. He waved his hand from side to side before he reached behind his back and retrieved a sack, rummaging through the contents, his worldly possessions, no doubt.

At last he removed an old shirt from the satchel, the rag mostly tattered. He ripped it even more, knotting the ends until he'd fashioned a long rope. He approached her, indicating he wanted to loop the rope around her.

"No!"

She smacked his hand.

Startled, he jumped.

"Get away!" she cried.

Madeline groped the palm trees, staggering deeper into the woods.

The boy was mad! He wanted to hold her captive. He'd watched her rise from the water, a fabled mermaid, and he intended to keep her, like treasure. Or perhaps he desired a friend? Perhaps he was just lonely?

Still, he was mad. She would *not* be bound like a slave. She had to find William. She had to find her grandfather. And she had to get off this cursed island! How had she misjudged the boy? How had she missed the madness in him?

"Ma-Maddie."

He uttered her name. He wasn't mute after all. And there was something about the inflection in his voice that inspired her to listen.

She glimpsed over her shoulder.

He remained a short distance away, lifting the rope. "Help," he said. "I help."

"No, I don't want your *help*."

"Maddie," he said again, his tone almost chastising. "You need help."

He pointed at his ribs, frowning.

And then it struck her: dressing, not rope. He had made dressing for her broken ribs, not rope for tying her hands.

She sighed and leaned against a tree. "Yes, help."

He humphed and trudged through the

undergrowth. As he reached her side, he motioned for her to lift her arms, and then bound her ribs with the dressing. The binding worked like a splint, immobilizing the fractured area, making it easier for her to breathe . . . though it still ached like damnation.

"Thank you." she smiled. "For help."

He nodded.

Thy boy was intelligent. And kind. A little dictatorial. But he *was* a young man. She had not misjudged him. And if she ever returned to England, she would take him home with her.

"Well, who do we have here?"

Madeline bristled at the smooth yet callous voice. Slowly the fine hairs on her body spiked, and her breath quickened in uneven rasps.

First, she shifted her wide eyes sidelong. Then, she peeked around the tree, stifling a scream.

Three toughened men stood in the thicket, decked with gleaming pistols and daggers, but it was the cutthroat in the middle who'd strangled her voice. He was taller than the rest, about thirty years old, his hair as black as iron, his eyes as blue as a tropical sea—but cold. Oh, so cold. He had a long black beard and a strapping build, but his entire expression rested in his eyes. The eyes of a devil.

"Take her," he ordered, the obvious leader of the group.

The others flanking him stepped forward. The brave, or perhaps foolish, boy pounced in front of her, fists raised. With heartless laughter, the brutes shoved him aside, sending him headlong into the dirt.

"No!" roared the devil. "I want the boy, too." His steely gaze narrowed on the prostrated youth. "He owes me a pretty penny."

In obedience, one ruffian scruffed the child and hoisted him to his feet, while the other grabbed her arm and dragged her deeper into the jungle.

Kidnapped, she thought. By pirates. Just like her grandfather. But as she passed the black devil, she shuddered, for the look he gave her told her he wouldn't be holding her for ransom . . . that he had a far worse fate for her in mind.

CHAPTER 20

S he's hurt," said Edmund, crouching beside the marks in the sand. He traced his fingers through the long trails, ruminating. "Looks like she dragged herself."

William scrunched, then flexed his blistered hands, a restless energy coursing through his veins. "How do you know it's Maddie? And not a tar?"

Edmund pointed up ahead. "Small footsteps there. Feminine." He edged closer to the prints. "Two sets. Someone helped her."

"Or abducted her," he gritted, his heart thundering.

The island was probably teeming with pirates. William grabbed the knife tucked into the waistband of his trousers and followed the footprints toward the jungle.

His brother lingered, gazing across the sea, and it wasn't difficult to imagine his torturous thoughts. William suffered them, too.

"She's alive, Eddie" he assured him, referring to his brother's wife. "They're all alive."

Edmund turned back to him, nodding. "I know. I

trust James. He'll protect her, all of them, with his life."

"He will."

Of that, at least, William was sure.

"This way," said Edmund, taking the lead.

He scrutinized the broken palms, locating a trail. He was in his element as an investigator, thought William, grateful for his help. All of his brothers had found their true callings. William just hadn't realized how well their new lives suited them until now, when their combined skills as hunters and healers were fully brought to light.

Edmund stilled. "There was a struggle."

"What?"

"Here," said Edmund, scouring the terrain. "Several men took her." He quickly found an abandoned, shabby-looking sack. "And the one who helped her." Rifling through the sack, he removed small articles of clothing. "A boy."

William tightened his grip on the knife, blood roaring in his ears. "Head back to camp," he ordered. "Gather the crew, all fit men, and as many weapons as you can find. Come after me. I'll follow the trail."

"Alone?"

"I have to go after her *now*."

"You're outnumbered and poorly armed."

"I can't wait." He started through the jungle. "If they hurt her . . ."

"But—"

"That's an order, lieutenant!"

"Aye, Captain."

He heard his brother's compliance at the back of

his mind as the two separated: Edmund to fetch reinforcements, and William to slit the throat of any man who laid a hand on his wife.

~ * ~

Madeline sat on the dirt floor of a hut, her wrists bound to a wood post. The boy was fastened to it, as well, and together they endured the discomfort, positioned back to back.

A breeze spiraled into the room through the open door, cooling her fevered flesh. Her heart had not stopped hammering since the abduction. She scanned the pirate camp outside, noted the sloop moored in the secluded bay, the jolly roger raised and flickering in the wind. An ideal hiding place, she thought with a measure of panic. But William would come for her. If he'd survived . . .

No. He had survived the wreck. And he would come for her. She believed in miracles. She had already found the pirates holding her grandfather hostage. Or they had found her, to be accurate. But where was her grandfather? Had something happened to him before she'd reached the island? And where was William? His crew? James?

Where *was* her miracle?

"Looking for someone?"

She'd tried her damnedest to ignore the black devil, seated in a wicker chair, arms folded across his chest, boots planted on a stool. She sensed his predatory gaze on her and shuddered in disgust.

The boy squeezed her hand, and she remembered she was not alone. She had to protect the lad. She had to locate her grandfather. And as soon as William came for her, she had to get the hell off the island.

But she couldn't let the pirate lord know her true identity, that she was the granddaughter of his captive, Sir Richard McNeal. The devil would expect the ten-thousand-pound ransom — which she hadn't brought.

Curse the storm! If it hadn't interfered with her journey, she'd be aboard the *Nemesis* right now, rescuing her grandfather, safe at her husband's side.

"I'm looking for my husband," she answered primly, warning him she was a married woman, not a whore for sale.

The boy stiffened.

The pirate offered a smirk. "Husband, eh?"

"Captain William Hawkins of the Royal Navy."

The navy was the bane of every pirate, she thought, hoping to frighten the black devil and secure their releases.

The pirate lord appeared thoughtful. "Hawkins?"

He had heard of her husband? Splendid! "Aye, Captain Hawkins."

He suddenly spat on the ground.

She jerked at the unexpected movement.

"I despise the Royal Navy." He lifted his boots from the stool, leaning toward her. "What is the fucking navy doing on my little island?"

With his black beard and livid blue eyes, he looked like a fallen angel — ready to break her neck. She found it hard to breathe and straightened her spine, but her bust lifted, too, attracting his loathsome attention.

"Not yet, sweetheart."

She quickly hunched her shoulders.

He got off the wicker chair so fast, it smashed to the ground. Crouching at her side, he snarled, "The navy, bitch. What is she doing here?"

The boy struggled at her backside.

The pirate smacked him upside the head. "Quiet, boy!"

The resounding "whack" across the boy's skull made *her* wince with pain—and her blood boil with rage.

"Coward," she whispered.

She could feel his breath on her skin. "What was that?"

Slowly she turned her head sidelong 'til their noses were level. "I called you a coward."

There was something about the shade of his cruel eyes that evoked familiarity, and for a moment, she thought she had met him before that day.

"Who are you?" she wondered.

"A coward," he said in a tight vein.

"What is your name?"

His fingers slithered up her throat, stroking her. "I have no name." He admired her a moment, tracing his knuckle over her chin. "I like your spirit, lass. You'll fetch me a good sum at the market."

"What market?" she rasped.

"The flesh market, of course." He dropped his hand, glaring at her. "This boy you're so eager to protect cost me ten thousand pounds."

She gasped. The same amount as the ransom?

"How?" she demanded.

"He released my captive: an old lord worth a great sum."

Her grandfather? The boy had saved her

grandfather? Her grandfather *was* alive!

Madeline stifled the storm of emotions swelling in her breast. If she shed a single tear or trembled in any way, she'd stoke the pirate's suspicions even more.

In a flat voice, she said, "A pity."

"For you, aye. I should salvage most of what I lost with you, sweetheart." His fingers reached for her throat again, but this time his grip wasn't gentle; he pinched her airway. "I'll ask one last time. What is the navy doing here?"

She croaked, "We washed ashore during the storm."

"I don't believe in coincidence." His grip tightened. "Try again, sweetheart, before I crush your gullet."

"My husband's really more of a privateer," she wheezed next, about to black out.

But then she sighted a flash of light. At first, she thought it a glimmering image of heaven, but when the black devil released her throat, and her starved lungs expanded with air, she focused on the light again — and found it a reflection off a steel blade.

A bruised hand held the knife firmly against the pirate's neck, so tight in fact, blood seeped from the wound already forming.

Madeline, still dazed, followed the battered hand to its arm and shoulder, and her eyes welled with tears at the brilliant sight of William.

"Get away from my wife," came the lethal order.

With his hair twisted in William's grip and his jugular exposed, the black devil had no choice but to obey the command. He lifted his arms in surrender and eased to his feet, slowly backing away from her — though his cruel gaze never left her face.

"Fire!" hollered the other pirates. "Fire, Captain!"

Madeline glanced out the door and noticed the smoke wafting from the sloop.

"You set my ship on fire?" the brigand growled.

"A necessary distraction," from William.

As the sailors dashed toward the burning sloop, the camp cleared.

William quickly divested the pirate captain of his many weapons, tossing them to the ground. A short blade landed right beside her hands.

"Cut yourself free, Maddie," he instructed, still keeping the pirate's throat in check.

Though her hands were numb, Madeline sawed at the rope with all her might. The boy took the blade from her after a while and finished the job, the last knot finally snapping away.

Such blessed relief, she thought, rubbing her aching arms and wrists. Blood pooled back into her extremities, and though her feet and hands prickled with the sensation of stabbing pins, she still wobbled to a stand.

The boy snatched a pistol from the floor and aimed it at the pirate. Madeline armed herself with another, giving William the opportunity to push the corsair against the wood post and lash him to it.

But before he looped the final knot, the pirate revealed a hidden leather strap around his wrist, tucked under his shirt.

"William!" she cried. "Look out!"

But the brigand was too quick. He swiped the concealed blade from his wrist — and shoved it into

William's belly.

Madeline screamed.

William staggered, then dropped to his knees, griping the handle, stunned, as blood pooled around his fingers.

She kneeled behind him, cradling his head as he toppled to the ground. "Oh, God! *No!*"

His lashes flickered. Blood seeped from the deep wound in his gut . . . and soon from the corner of his lips.

As she sobbed, the black devil shook the loosened rope off his hands and bounded toward the boy, knocking him aside and reclaiming his pistol.

He aimed it at William.

Madeline quickly lifted her gun, shooting first, but the wayward bullet hit the wall, her hand trembling, her eyes blinded with tears.

The fiend aimed again . . . when a shadow loomed over the hut, engulfing the entire structure. The panicked shouts from the other pirates also captured the blackguard's notice, and he glanced outside, his eyes widening as the *Bonny Meg* entered the bay, all twenty of her cannons aimed at the camp.

After a moment of hesitation, the pirate captain released a slew of curses and headed for the door, but he paused in the frame, his gaze on fire, his expression clear: *you will pay for this.*

Then he disappeared into the jungle.

Madeline dropped the pistol. The boy crouched beside her, covering her husband's gushing wound with a cloth he'd found, stymieing the blood flow.

"William," she whispered, her voice haggard.

"Maddie," he rasped.

She lowered her head and kissed him, his lips already growing cold, and her heart twisted with unbearable anguish. "I'm not ready to say farewell, luv."

She would never be prepared to say goodbye, to part from him forever, but she also hadn't expected his demise to be so soon. Or so violent.

"Shhh," he soothed, wrapping his hand around the back of her neck, holding her close. "It's better this way, Maddie. I . . . I always wanted to go like this, in battle."

"But what will I do without you?"

His beautiful blue eyes turned glassy with tears. "Live," he pressed her. "Live for me. Oh, Christ." He grimaced. "I wish . . . I wish I had met you sooner. I wish I had *lived* sooner. These last two months . . . Maddie, thank you." His color paled. As he weakened, his hand slipped from her neck, and he whispered, "I love you," before he went still, so very still.

"William?" Her voice cracked, "William, *please*, don't go."

Captain James Hawkins soon entered the hut, flanked by his younger brothers, Edmund and Quincy. Their sister, Belle, and her husband were not far behind, and Madeline shuddered with relief to learn the family and crew had survived the storm . . . all except for William.

"H-he's dying, James," she stuttered, a numbness coming over her. "My husband's dying."

Quincy quickly took the boy's place at William's side and peeled back the blood-soaked cloth to examine the knife wound. The blade still embedded in his brother's innards, Quincy features fell. "I can't help him."

Quiet followed his hopeless remark.

"He's already lost too much blood," said Quincy, his voice wavering. "And if I extract the knife, it will only hasten his death. He'll bleed out even faster."

Edmund dropped next to his brother, Belle followed suit. The somber air in the room was stifling, making it hard for Madeline to breathe. She both gasped and sobbed at the unbelievable realization: there was no miracle.

She crumpled over her husband, bussed his sweet lips again and again, holding him until he took his last, struggling breath.

James remained standing, stone hard, fisting and unfisting his hands. "Who did this, Maddie?"

"The pirate captain," she whimpered. "When your ship appeared in the bay, he ran into the jungle."

James roared orders to his crew, demanding they search the island for the elusive cutthroat. "We'll find him. And then I'll kill him."

The boy suddenly tugged on James's arm.

"Who the devil are you?"

Madeline pleaded, "Be kind, James. The boy saved my grandfather's life. He released him from captivity. Oh, God! My poor grandfather. He's somewhere on the island, too."

James issued another order to locate the old man.

But the boy seemed frantic, still pulling on James's arm.

"What, damnit?"

As the boy motioned for James to drop his ear, the

surly captain growled before lowering his head, but whatever the lad had whispered turned the captain's face a burning red.

"Don't tell tales, boy." And he boxed his ear, good and hard. "A man's dying."

The youth rubbed his sore ear, then kicked James in the shin. Cursing, James hunched forward, and the boy again flooded the captain's ear with a calliopean of frantic words. Madeline wasn't able to decipher them, but when the captain's expression changed, even lightened, her heart pounded with renewed vigor — and hope.

"What is it?" she demanded. "What did he say, James?"

After a thoughtful pause, James ordered, "Fetch that blanket, Quincy."

Quincy snatched the cotton sheet and draped it over William.

"No," snapped James. "Lay it on the ground and place William over it."

Quincy wrinkled his brow. "Why?"

"We're taking him into the jungle."

"Are you mad, James? If we move him, he'll die even sooner."

"I know."

"Then what the hell are you doing?" shouted Quincy.

"I haven't a fucking idea!" he thundered in return. "Just pick him up. And follow the boy."

CHAPTER 21

H ere," said James, heaving with fatigue. "Set him down beside the water."

After his exhausted brothers lowered William on the ground, Madeline rushed to his side. She stroked his cheek, cold as ice, and quickly lowered her ear to his breast. His chest lifted ever so slightly, a gurgling sound in his lungs. He was still breathing . . . barely breathing.

She looked around the jungle, the small pool of water. The palms hovered like a roof over the secluded spot, darkening the area so even sunlight couldn't penetrate the brush. It was so remote, so macabre. Why had they put her husband through such unnecessary pain? Hastened his death even with the arduous hike?

"Why did we bring him here?" she demanded, her voice cracking with grief.

Her sister-in-law squeezed her shoulder in support, her features just as hurt and confused.

James rubbed the back of his neck, doubtful, furious even. He pointed toward the boy and said in a stiff tone, "Ask your grandfather."

Madeline stared at the lad, bewildered. He

shrugged and smiled. And that smile brightened his eyes . . . his eyes.

"No," said Madeline, shaking her head, frantic. "No."

"Hullo, lass," he said.

And she covered her mouth at the familiar sound of his throaty burr. "Grandfather? What . . . happened . . . ?"

"I found it, lass." He stepped toward the pool and hunched beside it. "I finally found it . . . The Fountain 'o Youth." He cocked his head. "Look."

Her every bone trembling, Madeline leaned over her husband and stared into the small round pool, her eyes gaping. The water whirled into a black void and twinkled like stars in the heavens. Faraway lights collided in the void, unheard of worlds.

"We have to put him in the healing water, lass."

Her heart spasmed. "But he'll turn into a boy."

An image flashed in her mind: a child with unruly black hair and brilliant blue eyes — her husband? But he would live, she thought next. And he would grow again. Into a man. She would be a much older woman, but . . .

"I waded in the water too long," said the boy . . . her grandfather. "I floated until I shrunk an' almost drowned in my clothes. Don't keep him in the pool too long, just until the wound heals."

"Yes," she sobbed. "Yes!"

She had her miracle.

"The knife," said Quincy, reaching for it.

She stayed his hand. "No, I'll remove it." After a fortifying breath, she interlocked her fingers over the blade's handle and yanked the steel from William's belly.

His blood roiled and poured from the opened wound.

"Quickly." Madeline skirted aside, tossing the knife. "Place him in the water."

James and the duke took his legs, Quincy and Edmund his arms. Gently they settled him into the pool.

The family looked on as William floated in the water, swirling in the same counterclockwise direction as the mysterious current. The pool filled with his blood. The water lapped all around him.

Madeline's heart tightened as she watched the fatal wound slowly close.

"Fetch him," ordered James.

"No!" she cried. "Not yet."

"Why?"

"What about his illness? The wound in his belly is healed, but his sickness?"

James raked his hand through his hair. "How long do we leave him in there? Until he's a babe?"

She glanced at the scar on her husband's chest. "Did he fall ill before or after he was shot?"

"After," said Quincy.

"Are you sure?"

He bobbed his head. "Aye."

"Then we wait until the scar is gone, to the time *before* he was sick."

"Fine," gritted James.

It was a minute later the scar across William's chest shriveled and a bullet popped out, sucked into the whirlpool.

"Now!" shouted Madeline.

The brothers grabbed his feet and dragged him to the pool's edge before hoisting him from the water.

Madeline crouched at her husband's side, blood pounding in her ears. He remained so still, lifeless. "William?" She rocked his shoulder. "William?"

"What's wrong?" from Edmund. "Is he dead?"

Quincy dropped beside his brother and placed his ear over the man's chest. "No, he's breathing."

"The water is very comforting," said her grandfather, wedging his scrawny arms between her giant brothers-in-law. "I also fell asleep in it, remember?"

He then hunkered—and poked William in the eye.

William shot up, cursing and clutching his eye.

"Oh, thank God!" the family erupted in unmatched delight.

Her heart about to burst with pleasure, Madeline curled her arms around her husband's neck and sobbed, then smothered him with kisses and sobbed again.

When his strong arms circled her waist, and cradled her in a tender embrace, Madeline sobbed even harder until she gasped for breath.

"Easy, Maddie," came his husky voice, a soothing balm. "I'm here."

And he was. He was really here!

She pinched his hair and buried her lips in his ear, "I love you, William."

"And I love you." He bussed her neck. "What the hell happened to me?"

She half chuckled, half groaned. "We'll tell you on the journey back to the *Bonny Meg* . . . though I don't know if you'll believe us."

William lifted her to her feet and looked around at all the beaming faces, obviously bemused.

Her grandfather approached her. "Do you want to step into the healing water, lass? Mend your broken ribs?"

"Maddie." Her husband wrapped her in his arms again, stroked her cheek. "You're hurt?"

"No," she insisted. "I'm fine."

Her grandfather furrowed his brow. "Maddie?"

"I don't want to go into the water." If she entered the pool, her fractures would disappear . . . but so might the babe in her belly. "I'll heal in time. We've taken enough from the pool."

Quincy dipped his finger in the fountain. "I should bottle this, take it home to England. It would do so much good."

"Ye can't take the water," warned her grandfather, gripping his hand. "I tried, as well, to study it, but the island quaked like an earth tremor. The water must stay on the island."

A heavy sigh from Quincy. "What a pity."

A moment of thoughtful silence passed.

"Come," said James. "Let's go home."

~ * ~

Madeline watched her husband from a short distance. He stood alone at the starboard rail, his hair ruffled by the breeze, his shirt billowing with each gust of wind. The sun was slowly setting below the horizon, a fiery red, while brilliant streaks of pink and purple reached toward the heavens. To the east, a midnight blue already covered the hemisphere, stars twinkling in jewel-like glory.

She felt as if she was crossing between two worlds. Her life would never be the same again. She now had a husband. A twelve-year-old grandfather to raise. A babe on the way. A family.

"Care to join me, Maddie?"

He asked the question without even turning his head, aware of her presence, and a swell of emotion filled her breast at the thought that he sensed her so intimately, that their bond was so strong.

She neared him in quickened strides. His arms opened for her. In a moment she was sheltered in his embrace, his chest against her back, his cheek resting against her temple.

She gazed at the sunset with him. "It's beautiful, isn't it?"

"I feel like I'm seeing it for the first time," he returned, the awe in his voice unmistakable.

"Perhaps you are," she offered. "You have new eyes, a new heart."

He bussed her cheek. "I have you," he murmured.

She shuddered. "How are you headaches?"

"Gone."

"And the bleedings?"

"Stopped."

She sighed, content for now, but . . . "Do you think your illness will ever return?"

"I don't know. And I don't want you to worry, Maddie. Life is too short." Her breath hitched as he stroked her belly. "Too sweet to waste on idle troubles."

"You know about the babe?"

"I couldn't think of another reason why you wouldn't enter the healing waters."

She cupped his hand. "I thought I might lose the child. Quincy said my ribs will heal in three to six weeks. And there's no danger to the babe."

"You should rest, Maddie."

As he pulled away from her, she clinched his hand even tighter. "No, I've been in bed all day. I want to be with you."

He cradled her again, whispering, "Stubborn woman."

She smiled. "Thank you."

A low chuckle tickled her ear. "I suppose I shall never have an orderly life again."

"I would wager on that." A pause, then, "What will our new life look like, William?"

"First, we'll marry again. A legal ceremony with a minister. Then I'll sell the bachelor house in St. James's and find us a respectable home, perhaps Mayfair."

She stiffened.

"What's wrong, Maddie?"

"Would you mind if we lived in my grandfather's house?"

He cringed. "Aye, I would."

"I know it's eccentric, but it would please me, and him, to live there. It's home."

After a loud sigh and an incoherent muttering, he relented with, "I might be persuaded to raise our child in that beastly place *if* you redecorate."

Madeline grinned. "I'll pack up the shrunken heads, I promise."

"Hmm."

"And Grandfather? He will stay with us, won't he?"

Her grandfather had the wisdom of a seasoned captain and explorer. She couldn't bear the thought of treating him as a child and sending him off to a boy's college.

"Of course," said William. "We'll introduce him as our ward or adopted son."

She glanced over her shoulder and spotted her grandfather. He was seated on the steps of the poop, scribbling in a notebook, writing about his latest adventure, no doubt, and another smile tugged at her lips, for she imagined him on many more adventures . . . though she'd have to set some ground rules while he still resembled a child.

"But no one can know his true identity, Maddie. Sir Richard McNeal must remain lost at sea."

"Yes." Her smile faded. "Like so many others."

They had lost three crew members in the storm: the helmsman, the first lieutenant, and another shipman. A few other tars, missing after the wreck, were later located on the island.

"What will become of their families?" she wondered with a heavy heart.

"I will look after them," he assured her.

"Good. I just wish . . ."

"Shhh, I know. But my men loved the sea, Maddie. They accepted her riches — and her risks."

As Madeline thrummed her husband's hand, his brothers and their wives, followed by his sister and her husband, joined them at the *Bonny Meg*'s starboard rail. Together the entire family gazed out at sea before Captain James Hawkins broke the silence with a tart:

"I only wish I'd strangled the bastard before we'd

left the island."

His blood lust evoked several chuckles and a few grunts of agreement from his kin. The so-called "bastard" was the pirate captain that'd stabbed her husband before disappearing into the jungle. Despite their best efforts, the crew of the *Nemesis* and *Bonny Meg* had been unable to locate him. The black devil had likely retreated to a secret haven: a cave or underground tunnel perhaps.

In any case, the pirate lord's crew had been rounded up and delivered to the authorities of the nearest military port, where several ships were then dispatched in search of the elusive rogue. The rigs would remain off the island's coast until starvation or sheer isolation rooted the notorious devil from hiding.

Madeline shuddered at the memory of him even now. She could still feel his steely fingers gripping her throat, squeezing her airway. She could still see his merciless blue eyes, so cold and cutting . . . but the dark images flittered away as her husband bussed her temple and stroked her arms, an unshakable warmth settling throughout her soul.

"I'm sorry, James," said Madeline. "But if the bastard is ever discovered, I intend to strangle him myself."

The captain lifted an amused brow. "You'd make an excellent pirate, Lady Madeline."

"Thank you," she quipped.

William groaned. "Do not encourage my wife." He whispered, "She's already stolen everything from me."

At his sultry voice, Madeline shivered . . . then

gasped. A bloom appeared between his hands, a tropical flower. Where had he concealed the bright red blossom? Had one of his siblings passed it to him?

Before she'd uttered a startled remark, her husband gingerly tucked the flower behind her ear. "I've been meaning to do that since we first set sail, Maddie."

"But how?"

"A miracle, of course . . . like you, luv."

And then the "why" and "how" mattered naught anymore, for some things were meant to remain a mystery, she realized . . . including her love for one dashing pirate.

turn the page for a bonus novella
ALL I WANT FOR CHRISTMAS IS A PIRATE

ALEXANDRA BENEDICT

*All I Want for Christmas
is a Pirate*

CHAPTER 1
Mirabelle

England, 1827

Mirabelle, Duchess of Wembury, sat on the window seat, watching the snowflakes fall gently to the ground. The quiet before the storm, she mused, as her tempestuous family was about to descend on the castle for Christmas dinner.

A roasting fire crackled behind her, the sitting room alight with lamps and candles. Fresh greenery had been brought into the keep to adorn the mantle, and the distinct scent of pine filled the air.

Mirabelle inhaled a deep breath. Pine and oranges and lemons, all nestled together, a festive display of colors and aromas to tantalize the senses. She had come to love this time of year. She especially reveled in the few still moments just before the guests arrived.

A tall figure appeared in the doorframe, reflected in the glass, and a different kind of warmth settled over her. It was not an outward fire, penetrating through flesh and bone, rather an inward one, radiating from the center of her soul. The heat spread through every part of her, and she shuddered with delight. Her husband still affected her in a profound way. She wondered if her response to him would ever change. She hoped not.

Mirabelle turned away from the window and smiled. "Good evening, Your Grace."

Damian Westmore, Duke of Wembury, and the former "Duke of Rogues," returned her smile with a sensual one of his own, proving he hadn't quite retired his notorious epithet.

"It would be an even better evening," he said in a low voice, "if it was just the two of us for dinner."

Again a prickling sensation skimmed across her skin, spiking the fine hairs on her arms. From the first night she had met him aboard her family's ship, Mirabelle had known Damian would change her life forever. She hadn't wanted to believe it then, had tried desperately to fight her feelings for him, but her love for the duke would not be ignored, much less denied. She was grateful her fear and stubbornness had not won out. Otherwise, she would have missed the last six wonderful years of her life.

"Give me treat," demanded Henry.

"No, it's mine," cried his five-year-old sister, Alice, holding up a custard tart.

Henry toddled into the sitting room after his sister, both dressed in their long white sleeping gowns. He pursed his two-year-old lips, whimpered, then belted a wail that shook the stone fortress.

In that instant, Mirabelle sighed, her seductive play with her husband shattered. Damian tried not to laugh, but humor glistened in the pools of his dark blue eyes. He was really much too lax with the children, she thought. They were growing into hobgoblins.

In her most authoritative voice, Mirabelle demanded, "Alice. Henry. Why aren't you both in bed?"

The commotion stopped and two sheepish gazes rested on the duchess. The children had taken after Mirabelle with their fair locks and golden eyes, but their wild temperaments . . . those *must* have come from their father.

"We wanted to see our uncles," said Alice with the innocence of a babe.

But Mirabelle had learned her daughter was far more intelligent and mischievous than her beguiling eyes revealed. "Oh, really? And it had nothing to do with stealing tarts from the kitchen?"

The impertinent girl actually licked the custard before avowing, "Not a bit, Mama."

With a sigh, Mirabelle stood up from the window seat and stretched out her hand. "Give me the tart."

The girl pouted. "But our uncles?"

"You will see your uncles in the morning. Give me the tart, Alice. Now."

Alice made a moue before she sulkily pressed the tart into her mother's palm—custard side down.

Mirabelle gasped. "Alice!"

The two sprites dashed from the room, well, Henry waddled, both shouting, "Goodnight, Papa! 'Night, Mama!"

Mirabelle stared at her husband, incredulous. "That hoyden!"

The duke removed a kerchief from his coat pocket, his lips twitching as he approached his wife. "We've both done much worse as children."

"How can you laugh? She's turning into a—"

"Pirate? Like her mother?"

Mirabelle glared at her husband as he removed the mushy tart from her hand, setting it aside on a nearby table.

"Do *not* say that word," she hissed. "You know I don't want Alice to learn about my past."

If the rebellious girl discovered her mother *and* all four of her uncles had once been pirates, there would be no end to her obstinacy.

"Whatever pleases you, my love," he murmured, leaning forward.

Mirabelle expected her husband to wipe the custard from her palm with the kerchief, but he brought her hand to his sensuous lips instead.

Her breath hitched. His hot tongue laved the creamy sauce from her skin, sending shivers of unanticipated pleasure down her spine.

"The tart tastes far better served on you, my dear."

The rogue.

And yet she didn't protest the diversion. Her frustration softened. She closed her eyes, lost in the intimate moment with her husband. "I think Alice had the right idea. You and I should steal a few tarts from the kitchen—for later tonight."

Damian chuckled, a throaty sound, before he bussed her lips, feather soft, sugary vanilla on his breath.

"Do you ever think about having more children?"

she wondered.

His smile dropped. "No."

"Really?" She took the kerchief from his fingers and wiped her hand. "I sometimes think—"

"No," he said again, his features taut. "No more children, Belle."

She wasn't surprised by his rigid response. She had come close to death giving birth to their son two years ago. It had taken her several months to recover from the trauma and many more months before her husband would touch her again. Even now, Damian refused to have any relations with her unless they took measures to block another pregnancy.

"I know it can be dangerous," she said softly. "But I grew up in a large family. I can't recount the trials we suffered or the joys we celebrated. And without the support of my brothers, life would've been even more difficult. I just want Alice and Henry to have the same fellowship."

"I know, Belle, but the children have us, their uncles, their cousins. They won't want for strong kinship."

"Yes, they have us, but my older brothers are so often at sea, while the youngest are newlyweds and just settling into marital life. Meanwhile, your brother and his children live near the coast." She sighed. "I wanted a big family under one roof."

"I'm sorry, Belle, but you and I will never have another child."

Her inherent, headstrong nature butted forth then, and she was prepared to challenge his autocratic ruling when the dong of the front bell echoed throughout the keep. "Hell's fire. They just had to be punctual. We'll discuss this matter at another time, Damian."

"The matter is decided, Belle."

"Damian—"

"I will not risk losing you again." His voice cracked, ever so slight. His eyes darkened, glistened, even. "I lie awake every night, watching you sleep, counting your breaths. I listen to your every movement as you roll under the sheets or murmur in your dreams. I smell the perfume on your skin, the life in your veins—and I will not tempt fate again, not even to have another child as beautiful as you."

Tears gathered in her eyes, the briny moisture spilling down her cheeks. "Damian, I—I had no idea you felt this way." She wrapped her arms around her husband's neck and squeezed him tight. "I don't want you to live in fear of losing me," she whispered.

"I don't think that fear will ever leave me," he returned, his voice hoarse with emotion. "But I will do everything in my power to protect you."

At his heartfelt confession, Mirabelle knew she would never have another babe. A part of her mourned the thought, but another part of her was moved beyond measure by the depth of her husband's love for her.

"I understand," she assured him, dabbing at her eyes. "And as you said, we shouldn't tempt fate. We might just have another hoyden."

A robust laugh rumbled in the duke's chest. "I love you, Belle."

"And I love you."

Soon a resounding hail of booted footsteps and

spirited voices filled the grand hall.

"You will behave, I trust," she admonished her husband. "I don't want any rows between you and my brothers."

Damian snorted, neither confirming nor denying her request. A man once titled the "Duke of Rogues" had not inspired confidence in her brothers, and they'd downright thought her mad for marrying the duke. But, as Mirabelle had learned, love was never sensible.

She hadn't a moment to upbraid her husband when her brother, Captain James Hawkins, entered the room.

The eldest at forty-two, James also had the most fearsome expression. It had wholly suited him when he'd roamed the high seas as the infamous pirate Black Hawk, but as a gentleman of high society and a respectable merchant captain, the long black hair tied in a queue and stormy blue eyes as threatening as the devil were a source of apprehension and gossip.

And yet those eyes softened when they fell on her, and she simpered, for she sensed his tender regard toward her. "Happy Christmas, James."

He opened his arms, and she walked into his embrace.

"How are you, Belle? Is the bounder treating you well?"

"Very well," she affirmed.

An exotic woman with dark brown hair, sharp brown eyes and a resplendent, brocade amber dress next stepped into the sitting room, her smile broad. "Happy Christmas, Belle."

Mirabelle returned the festive greeting and embraced her sister-in-law. Born and raised on the island of Jamaica, Sophia was a strong, spirited woman who matched her brother in every way. The couple had married over a year ago, and it was something of a sensation that the most forbidding of all her siblings had actually wed — and was happy.

"How was your journey?" asked Mirabelle.

"Uneventful," returned Sophia.

Mirabelle lifted a teasing brow. "No dalliances in the carriage, James?"

James balked at her outlandish remark, and damn if a little red hadn't crossed his wicked brow.

Sophia chuckled, a rich, husky sound, but her husband remained silent — and glowering.

"Now that's what I like to see," said Damian, crossing the room to greet his guests. "The infamous pirate speechless. Well done, Belle."

She winked at the duke. "And where are the others? At your heels, I hope?"

"Right at our heels," assured Sophia.

"I'll oversee the luggage, then," said Mirabelle.

Her family would be staying at the castle until Twelfth Night. She had prepared their usual rooms, but she wanted to make sure all the details were addressed. Besides, James needed a moment to regain his wits. The duchess had clearly not retired all of her piratical ways either.

CHAPTER 2
James

Captain James Hawkins stood in the middle of the dressing room in front of the full-length mirror—stark naked. He had changed out of his traveling clothes and was about to pull on his eveningwear, when a pair of seductive eyes trimmed with long, sooty lashes caressed him through the glass.

She could set him afire with just one scorching look. If anyone else had that sort of hold over him, he'd struggle for supremacy. But he was coming not to mind his wife's captivating influence.

James returned the woman's heated gaze. "Let down your hair, sweetheart."

A slow smile spread across her sensuous lips. She stepped into the dressing room from the adjoining bedchamber and approached him in a deliberate manner. He studied her every artful movement through the glass.

Sophia stopped behind him and wrapped her arms around his waist, her warm fingers raking the muscles of his abdomen, and when she pressed her wicked mouth against the curve of his spine, he groaned low in his throat.

"Later," she purred. "After dinner."

James closed his eyes and steadied his already quickened breath. If he didn't regain control of his senses, there would be no dinner, and he could just imagine his audacious sister barging into the room at the most importune moment, demanding to know the reason for their delay.

After recovering a measure of his unbridled lust, James opened his eyes. His wife was watching him with a smirk, ever aware of the power she had over him, and the witch was all but glowing with satisfaction. She took far too much pleasure in tormenting him, he thought, disgruntled.

"The family is informal, sweetheart. I'm sure no one will mind if you let loose your hair."

He loved her lush locks spilling over her backside, unfettered by combs and pins. Wild. Like her.

James remembered the first time he had met her in the untamed mountains of Jamaica. Cutting through the swirling mist and tangled brush, he had made his way to a ramshackle house in the peaks, searching for an old buccaneer who had once saved his father's life. But there, deep in paradise, James had also found Sophia, the pirate's daughter.

She had greeted him with the barrel of a pistol, her suspicious eyes peering at him over the flintlock, her thick tresses, like smooth cocoa, flowing over her shoulders in abundant waves.

"Black Hawk, I presume? My father's told me all about you."

At the stirring memory, James shuddered.

"I prefer to wear my hair up for dinner," she said

in a playful drawl, thwarting his desire.

He humphed. "If you're finished torturing me, woman, it's time I dressed for dinner."

She chuckled, a smoky chortle, before she slapped his arse and sashayed a few steps away. "I've been meaning to talk to you, James."

"What about?"

He pulled on his breeches as Sophia fetched him his linen shirt. He had no valet, detesting the pompous convention, but he'd grown rather fond of his wife's help in the manner of dressing—and disrobing.

She handed him the shirt. "I'm pregnant."

James froze with only one arm through a sleeve. A cold, rushing panic gripped him, and he stared at the woman as if she'd turned into a goat.

"James?"

"How?"

A dark brow quirked. "Really?"

"You are barren, woman," he growled.

Was she funning with him? She had the same damn smirk in her eyes. He couldn't tell if she was being sincere. She had always found a perverse titillation in making him miserable.

"I'm not amused, Sophia."

"Good." She folded her arms under her generous breasts. "I'm vexed about it, too. You just *had* to be so virile?"

She *was* winding him up, the witch. And with the worst possible jest. Sophia knew he didn't want any urchins. Ever. After the death of his mother, James had reared his siblings while their father had pirated at sea. Those had been the most difficult years of his life. And he was *done* nursing brats and raising hoydens. He sure as hell wasn't going to start another family at forty-bleeding-two years of age!

"Enough, Sophia. I'm in a piss poor mood now."

He yanked on the rest of his clothes, a vest and coat, and tied back his hair in a roughshod manner before stalking out of the dressing room. He sat on the edge of the bed, cramming his feet into his shoes, all the while glancing at Sophia askance.

The woman had yet to confess she was toying him. Her silence stretched. Her gaze remained fixed and unflinching. And James started to feel uneasy.

"You're barren," he repeated, making her ploy inconceivable.

Sophia was only twenty-eight years of age, a fertile period for most women, but she and James had met eight years ago, and their heated affair had never produced any offspring. After a torrid year together on the island, their affair had ended in a crushing blow that had soured him for years. And James wasn't naive. His sensual Sophia had taken other lovers in the time they'd been apart. But she had *never* had a pregnancy. And she had never used anything to block one because . . . She. Was. Barren.

"James," she said softly. "Haven't you noticed I was getting a little 'plump' in certain areas?"

He snorted, then murmured under his breath.

"What was that?" she demanded.

"I said, I noticed."

"And?"

"And I didn't think it wise to mention you were getting 'plump.' Besides, I adore your curves, you know that."

She smiled, her eyes smoldering. "What about our nights together? Haven't you noticed I've not pushed you away for the last three months?"

James paused, then frowned.

"I haven't had my menses in three months, James."

His heart started to pound. No. Impossible.

"But we don't want children," he rasped, suddenly strapped for breath.

Sophia had spent her youth caring for her mad father. She, like James, had no desire to take on more responsibility; they were both gratified with each other.

And it wasn't as if James disliked children. He adored his niece and nephew. But the brats were his sister's obligation. He just . . . He just couldn't do this. Not again.

Sophia sauntered toward the bed and settled beside him, slipping a comforting arm around his shoulders. "Shall I fetch you a bottle of rum?"

James dropped his head between his hands. "Blimey."

CHAPTER 3
Edmund

I do *not* believe you, Edmund Hawkins."

Edmund paused—about to stuff a tart into his mouth. He was ensconced in a dark corner of the castle's kitchen, tankard in one hand, pastry in the other. Sensing his wife's displeasure, he crammed the tart into his mouth then downed the wine before looking over his shoulder.

Amy was stunning: piqued, arms akimbo. Her long fair hair was rolled and twisted in a delicate crown on her head, while her flushed cheeks hinted at the fire in her soul. And her eyes, so vivid green, burrowed into him. But he never minded their striking stare. She always peered inside him, not at him, and he shuddered at the intimacy of her gaze— however vexed.

She had quite literally twirled into his life two years ago, sweeping across a stage in a gentleman's club, dancing, attired in white silk and coins, her face veiled—all except for those mysterious eyes. Her aristocratic life had been stolen from her. But she had found a way to survive in the dark world of the rookeries. And she had stirred his listless heart to life that night—and had been stirring it ever since.

"You look lovely, Amy."

"Bullocks." She waved aside the compliment, her bejeweled slipper tapping. "You're not dressed for dinner."

He glanced at his dusty travel clothes. Since arriving at the castle, he had paused to peck his sister on the cheek before making his way straight toward the kitchen. "I was hungry."

She huffed then joined him at the small table. "You are always hungry. But we're not heathens."

"I couldn't wait for dinner," was his grumbled excuse.

His wife's features sharpened even more. "And who is to blame for your empty stomach? If you hadn't spent the entire morning at Bow Street, you could have joined me for luncheon before we'd headed for the castle."

Edmund fell silent at the mention of the Bow Street Magistrates Office, his place of employment as an investigator. His quiet only ruffled his wife's temperament, and she demanded, "What is it?"

But he wouldn't ruin her evening and shrugged. "Nothing a'tall."

"What happened at Bow Street?" She grabbed his hand from across the table. "Tell me."

As her fingernails penetrated his skin, it was clear her night was already ruined, her anxiety roused, and he had no choice but to put her mind at ease, however difficult the task.

Slowly he covered her hand. "I received word,

Amy."

She paled. "Gravenhurst?"

A year ago, Lord Gravenhurst had almost murdered Amy. It'd been an act of revenge against her father, a duke, for sins committed when she was an innocent babe.

The memory still haunted Edmund. In vivid detail, he reflected on the moment he'd stormed the bedroom, witnessed the gut-churning sight of Amy's throat between the fiend's crushing hands.

He shuddered again—but with unshakeable fury. He had thrashed the son-of-a-bitch to within an inch of his life, rescued Amy, but the swine had escaped, disappeared.

Edmund and his fellow Bow Street Runners had hounded the elusive bastard for months, and now, finally, their search was at an end.

"He's dead, Amy."

She squeezed his hand ever tighter. "Are you sure?"

"A body was discovered at the base of a cliff." He refrained from the grisly details, like the broken limbs dashed against the rocks, the bloated flesh. "He committed suicide."

"And you're *sure* it's him?"

"Aye," he returned, caressing her quivering hand. "The body had laid on the beach for a few days, its features unrecognizable."

"Then—"

"No," he stopped her frantic thought. "His height, his clothes, his signet ring, even the papers in his coat pocket—*all* prove his identity. Gravenhurst is dead, I swear."

Her trembling fingers stilled. She sighed. A tear appeared in her eye, then another.

"It's over, Amy."

"I believe you. It's just . . ."

"What?"

She slipped her hand away, dabbed at her eyes. "He had such hate for Papa. He lived an angry, lonely life. He hurt me. And you. And for what?"

"I don't understand." He frowned. "Do you feel charitable toward the devil?"

"I feel sad," she said at last. "Such waste, Edmund. And for nothing. Nothing a'tall. In the end, Death."

Edmund lifted from his seat and kneeled beside her. "It was his choice, Amy."

"I know." Her gaze lighted on him, sparkled with an effervescence that took his breath away. "I just have so much love in my life. And I wish . . . I wish every lost soul could find it, too."

His heart seized at her unexpected confession. For so long, he had hunted the monster, surrounded his wife with trusted guards when he wasn't there to protect her himself. How many sleepless nights had he paced their bedroom, peering through the curtains, searching for a shadowy figure in the street? And now the monster was dead. And rather than rejoice with him, Amy pitied the bastard. She pitied him because he hadn't love . . . like her.

A finger brushed his cheek. "Is that a tear, Edmund?"

"Rubbish." He stuffed the sentiment into the bowel of his soul, but she never failed to inspire him with hope, to broaden his dreams and stretch his unending love for her.

He rasped, "I love you, Amy."

"And I you, Edmund."

A weight lifted from his shoulders. Fear regressed. And a lightness entered his body. She was safe. At last.

"We'll tell the others at dinner," he said, clearing his throat, gathering his wits. "They've been worried about us for such a long time."

"I don't want to spoil anyone's appetite. We'll share the news after dinner, I think." She then slipped her hand through his arm. "Let's get you dressed. I'm looking forward to a festive meal with my family."

He walked with her through the kitchen. "And, ah, not a word to my siblings about any rot, like tears."

"Oh?"

"I mean it, Amy," he growled.

She snuggled into his arm. "I will keep your secret, I promise. Can you imagine the shock should anyone discover you're not a notorious scoundrel but a good man with feeling?"

"Perish the thought, indeed."

CHAPTER 4
Quincy

The ballroom glimmered under a soft glow as Quincy Hawkins set alight the last candle. He waved the matchstick, extinguishing the flame before turning toward his radiant wife.

She stood a few yards away, wearing a golden gown, her expression coy, her leaf-green eyes shimmering under the resplendence. And while her elfin features might confuse any other man into believing her an otherworldly sprite, she was in fact a sensual woman with deep desires he never tired of pleasing.

Quincy extended his right hand. "Might I have this dance, sweet Holly?"

Her lips formed a sensuous smile. She curtsied with aplomb before taking his hand, and together they waltzed across the silent room.

"We danced this dance at the ball where we first met," she purred in an arousing manner.

"Bully to that," he murmured. "We first met in a gentleman's club."

Her strawberry-flaxen locks burned a darker

shade of red in the low light—as did her pinkening cheeks. "Yes, well, our first 'official' meeting was in a ballroom like this one."

"You'd already seen me naked by then."

The heat in her gaze slowly simmered. "I had, hadn't I?"

"Wench."

Her smile broadened. She had once detested that word, but since marrying him, she'd grown rather fond of it, and her tenderness toward the epithet demonstrated just how much their relationship had strengthened.

Quincy hadn't realized he'd been strapped for breath until a whoosh of air escaped his cramped lungs. His blood reeled as a precious memory overwhelmed him: the first time he'd set eyes upon Holly.

It had been a year ago, on Christmas Eve. She'd stumbled into his room at the bawdy house, mistaking him for her model. As the notorious *Lord H*, Holly had painted nudes to support herself. And when his bare arse had appeared in the underground artworld, Quincy had been convinced she'd ruined his life. Worse, he'd been forced to marry the wench in order to prevent a scandal and protect their reputations.

It was hard to imagine, but he'd once thought he'd never be happy with Holly, with any woman, really. He'd been obsessed with opium for ages, plagued by nightmares and saddled with guilt over past sins . . . luckily, his wily wife had seduced him, healed him, offered him hope.

Disarmed by the unruly emotions teeming inside

him, Quincy captured her soft mouth in a tight and sizzling kiss. She stumbled once, twice before regaining her footing, then lilted with him in harmony around the dance floor, their lips still locked in a passionate buss.

As his blood burned — too hot — he broke away from the kiss, rasping, "Happy Christmas, Holly."

Her voice fluttered. "Happy Christmas."

He needed to take his mind off the raw urges stirring within him, and offered, "Congratulations on the smashing success of your first exhibit."

Since retiring the pseudonym *Lord H*, Holly had taken up the more enigmatic initials *H. H* for Holly Hawkins. She had recently presented a collection of art incognito, unleased a new form of expression, in truth: a sort of nonrepresentational work instead of the usual objective art.

She snorted. "Half the critics despised my efforts."

"It doesn't matter if they love you or hate you, my dear, so long as it's one extreme or the other, so long as you're the subject of discussion, gossip, even."

She cocked her head, thoughtful. "I suppose."

"You are now an acclaimed artist. And your work will be in ever higher demand — just don't tell anyone you're a woman."

"I wouldn't dare." She made a moue. "I'd be declared an abomination. Any critic who'd respected my work would have to hide face for supporting a *woman* artist, while my detractors would revel in pompous approval, vindicated that my work was *not* art because of my sex."

At the rising pitch in her voice, he nuzzled her

brow in comfort. "I'm afraid *H.H* will remain a mystery to posterity . . . but your brilliant work will last forever."

"Thank you," she whispered. "And how goes your medical practice, Doctor Hawkins?"

"The suites are furnished and I have two official patients."

A slender brow arched. "Impressive."

He wasn't bothered by her teasing. A new "quacksalver" set up shop every day in Town. It would take time to earn the public's trust. And Quincy had time. Since boyhood, he'd possessed a fascination with the healing arts. He'd even trained as a surgeon aboard one of his brother's ships. But it wasn't until a few months ago, when he'd received his accreditation from the Royal College of Physicians, that he'd opened his own practice on Harley Street.

"In truth," he said, "I prefer working at the Royal Hospital for Incurables and the Royal Free Hospital in Hatton Gardens."

"Why?"

"The physicians there are little more than blacksmiths and barbers. The patients are desperate for help. And I intend to make changes in sanitation, nursing. I will still keep my private practice like any respectable doctor, but my work at the hospitals are far more meaningful."

"Because you have talented hands, my love."

Was that a double entendre?

As his blood smoldered again, he caressed her lithe fingers. "Would you trust me with your painter's hands?"

"I would trust you with every part of my body, including my heart."

His own heart pounded ever quicker, and their dance slowed to an idle undulation. "If you'd like me to perform a thorough examination, my love?"

She gasped. "We'll be late for dinner."

"Dinner be damned."

She paused, scraping her teeth over her plump bottom lip — then pulled him in for a heady kiss.

CHAPTER 5
William

Captain William Hawkins strolled through the castle, arm in arm with his wife. It was her first visit to the ancient fortress, and she'd been enchanted by its grotesque exterior and modern, illuminated interior. He'd showed her all the principal rooms. And now, there was just one hall left to tour.

"Last," he said with majestic flair, "is the library."

William opened the heavy oak door, revealing a vaulted ceiling with three stories of priceless tomes, and a giant globe in the middle of the room.

Madeline rushed toward it. "How marvelous!"

He had saved the library as the last stop on their jaunt, knowing it would bring her the greatest pleasure. And as she grazed her fingers over the circular map in wonder, and her emerald eyes sparkled with awe, his chest tightened.

Lady Madeline's Winters had entered his life several months ago, during his darkest hour. She was his miracle. She was also five months pregnant, possessed a wicked temper and always found a way to put him in a damnable position—but he still thanked heaven for her every day.

Her hand soon rested over a streak of isles in the Bahamas. "I don't see our island here."

Their "island" was one of many uncharted landmasses in the Caribbean: just a small outcrop of boulders, beach and jungle with no human habitation—and thus the perfect shelter for a band of pirates.

William's mood darkened as he remembered the buccaneers who'd kidnapped his wife, threatened her harm . . . and the pirate leader who'd stabbed him in the belly. The bloody island shouldn't hold any fond memories for him, but it's there they'd found a pool of healing water, water that had mended his lethal wounds and offered him a lifetime with Madeline.

Aye, it was "their" island: a secret, magical place.

William shut the door and approached his wife. "There are many lands left to find and explore, luv... but I'm afraid no one will ever see 'our' island on any map."

"What do you mean?"

"It's gone, Maddie."

Madeline blinked, bemused. "Gone? How can an island disappear?"

As a privateer in the Royal Navy's African Squadron, William was privy to reports from the Admiralty. He had recently learned that an island in the Bahamas—their island—had vanished.

While the pirate crew had been imprisoned by the authorities, their captain, a nameless devil, had eluded capture, and so the Royal Navy had routinely circled the island in search of the castaway captain, confidant deprivation would force him out of hiding—until one day they found the island missing.

"A few days ago, I came across a naval report, recounting yet another survey of the island in search of the elusive pirate captain."

"The fiend," she said in a tart voice.

William cupped her shoulders. "You don't have to worry about him anymore, Maddie. The island sank in the sea: an earthquake according to the report. And the pirate leader drowned with the island."

For a moment, she remained still. Soon, her ginger brown curls bobbed as she tapped her foot. "That coward!"

William arched a bow. "I beg your pardon?"

"He scuttled the island rather than face trial, rather than face *us* for his crimes."

"Maddie, I don't think an island—"

"Can sink? On purpose? Of course, it can, Will. Remember the healing waters?"

William strained his memory. He had so few images in his mind, mostly sentiments like, pain, dizziness, and then the sensation of warmth and comfort. "I don't understand, Maddie."

"After we removed you from the pool, your brother Quincy tried to bottle the healing water but was warned the island would tremble."

"Like an earthquake," he said, a vivid picture coming into his head.

"Aye." She sniffed. "That *fiend* disturbed the pool, sending the island to the bottom of the sea—and evading justice, of course."

"Perhaps you're right, Maddie."

"I know I'm right," she huffed. "I looked straight into his eyes, Will. I confronted a Coward."

As her features turned an even greater shade of red, he worried about her health and that of the babe's, drawing her into his arms and lulling her with an encompassing embrace.

"It's over, Maddie."

She sighed. "I wanted to watch him hang."

He groaned at her bloodthirsty response. "You're a dangerous woman to cross."

"Thank you."

"I'm not sure that was a compliment."

"I accept it as a compliment."

As her smile returned, he chuckled. "Are you hungry?"

"Famished."

He steered her toward the door, a protective arm around the small of her back. "I'm sure dinner is about to be served."

The couple sauntered through the corridors, making their way toward the dining hall. Inside, most of the family had already gathered around the large table. The duke and duchess ogled each other from across the heads of the table. James looked rather petulant, though Sophia rubbed his arm in assurance. Edmund and Amy were both quiet, but content. And moments later, Quincy and Holly rushed into the room, disheveled and blushing.

As William and Madeline took their seats, footmen served platters of freshly cooked fare and poured red wine into chalices.

William scooped his chalice and lifted to his feet. "I propose a toast."

The gesture unexpected, the family stared at him. After all, he was the most unspontaneous of the clan. At least, he used to be before he met his wife.

As soon as everyone had a cup in hand, he went on with, "To happily-ever-after. Though sometimes late, 'tis better than never."

"Here! Here!"

And amid the roar of celebrators, the ringing of chalices echoed throughout the castle.

CHAPTER 6
Drake . . . Junior

As Captain Drake Hawkins stood outside the
castle window, watching his half siblings
toast with disgusting cheerfulness, his
innards churned ever greater.

His horse snorted and sidestepped, sensing his
growing rage, and he swallowed the bile back down
his throat before the animal panicked.

"Wretched curs," he snarled.

They had stolen everything from him: his pirate
crew, his ship, his island—and his father, for Drake
Senior had loved his legitimate children far more than
his bastard son.

At the pain in his chest, he girded his muscles. It
was fucking unfair! They had betrayed their father,
turning into nobs, joining the royal navy—becoming
everything their father had despised. And *he*, the
loyal son was the outcast?

His eyes still pegged on his loathsome kin, Drake
twisted the reins of his horse around his hands so
tight, welts formed across his palms.

"I will destroy you all," he vowed, blood pooling

in his hands. "I will make you pay for what you've done to me . . . and to the memory of our father."

And with that final oath, Drake pulled on the reins, kicked his horse's flanks and galloped into the wintry darkness . . .

WELCOME!

Enter the sensual and swashbuckling world of The Hawkins Brothers: four dark and dangerous pirates who retire their wicked ways after their sister becomes a duchess. But can the rugged rogues enter high society in Regency England, masquerading as gentlemen? Or will their true identities be revealed?

Learn all about the sexy brigands by turning the page, but beware! The Hawkins Brothers just might steal your heart and never give it back.

MY HERO

Take the following personality quiz and find out which Hawkins brother is best suited to steam up your night!

1. On a warm and sunny day, I'd be outside:
A. On a nature walk
B. Gardening
C. Hosting a BBQ
D. Playing sports

2. At a dinner party, I'm most likely to drink:
A. Wine
B. Ginger Ale
C. Beer
D. Anything!

3. My favorite holiday is:
A. Valentine's Day
B. Christmas
C. Thanksgiving
D. Halloween

4. If I could go anywhere in the world, I'd visit:
A. Jamaica
B. Africa
C. Las Vegas
D. Ibiza, Spain

5. My idea of the perfect date is:
A. A late night picnic on the beach
B. An intimate dinner at a restaurant
C. Going to a football game
D. An evening of dancing

ANSWERS: MY HERO

Mostly As: James Hawkins
Captain James Hawkins, the infamous pirate leader Black Hawk, is the oldest of the Hawkins brood and wields the greatest brute strength. As the head of the family, he is saddled with responsibility and can prove stubborn at times as he struggles to keep his kin together and away from the gallows. He prizes loyalty above all other qualities and possesses a lusty appetite for life's simple pleasures. A true alpha male, he can communicate an order to a tar (or a desire to a woman) with just one piercing look. However, he also has a tender side, achingly soft at times, but well concealed. It is only in moments of great peace that he drops his iron front and lets the tenderness show.

See James Hawkins meet his match in *The Infamous Rogue* and *Mistress of Paradise*.

Mostly Bs: William Hawkins
William Hawkins is the second eldest and the most levelheaded of the Hawkins brood. Intelligent and even tempered, he can see both sides of a story clearly. He has a knack for settling a conflict before it gets out of hand, earning him the status of peacemaker in the tempestuous family. But William's sensibility leads to emotional indifference, making him a stranger to romantic love. Will the responsible William open his heart at last, and let the wild and stormy ways of love take root?

Find out in *How to Steal a Pirate's Heart*.

Mostly Cs: Edmund Hawkins

Hot-tempered Edmund Hawkins is the middle brother. He enjoys a big meal and a good round of fisticuffs. Secretive, he tends to keep to himself, talking only if he has something worthwhile to impart. He is content to let his older brothers rule the roost, while he searches for amusement elsewhere ... in London's underworld. Will the brooding Edmund find a woman who will bring out the champion in him?

Look for his emotional story in *The Notorious Scoundrel.*

Mostly Ds: Quincy Hawkins

The pup, Quincy Hawkins, is the youngest of the Hawkins brood and the most likely to get into scrapes. Charming and flirtatious, he makes the ladies swoon. He's always ready for fun or adventure—even if it lands him in the gaol. He's honest (too honest) and will always tell you what's on his mind. But the fun-loving rake possesses another, darker side. Personal demons lead him astray. Will he find a deep and enduring love to help him reconcile with his tortured past?

Don't miss his tale in *How to Seduce a Pirate.*

THE HAWKINS BROTHERS SERIES

Mistress of Paradise (prequel)

A dark and troubled soul, Captain James Hawkins seeks freedom from his tortured past as the infamous pirate, Black Hawk. But when he meets a seductive beauty on the island of Jamaica, he finds a passion greater than any foray at sea.

Sassy, fierce and independent, Sophia Dawson knows her heart's desire—and it's the sexy brigand who tempts her with promises of pleasure. In his arms she finds erotic delight and respite from duty as her mad father's caretaker.

But a storm lurks on the horizon as the couple's heated affair attracts scorn from the islanders. Will James and Sophia weather the brutal tempest . . . or will there be trouble in paradise?

To see if James and Sophia find love in each other's arms again, read their story in *The Infamous Rogue*, available now from Avon Books

The Infamous Rogue (book one)

The daughter of a wealthy bandit, Sophia Dawson once lost herself in the arms of Black Hawk, the most infamous pirate ever to command the high seas. But now, determined to put her sinful past behind her, she prepares to enter society as the bride of a well-born nobleman who knows nothing of her scandalous youth. All goes according to plan until her ex-lover — now a respectable sea captain but just as handsome and dangerous as ever — appears and once again tempts her with desire.

From the moment he sees Sophia again, James Hawkins wants only one thing: revenge. He'll see to it that the reckless beauty pays for abandoning their heated affair. And so begins a battle of wills that can end only in utter ruin . . . or wicked surrender . . .

"The sexy, intriguing pirates Benedict introduced in Too Great a Temptation return as the heroes of their own series. But men like these need heroines to match, and Benedict has created a smart and sassy spitfire of a woman to add spice and heat to a tale filled with biting repartee and passionate drama. You'll relish this lively high-seas romp."

Romantic Times Book Reviews
on *The Infamous Rogue*, Also a Reviewer's Choice Nominee for Best Historical Romantic Adventure

The Notorious Scoundrel (book two)

Like an irresistible siren, the veiled dancer with the bewitching green eyes lures dukes and earls into London's underworld to see her dance — and succumb to her spell. Some says she's a princess, but only one man knows her darkest secret.

She is Amy Peel, an orphan from the city's rookeries, and she believes the bold rogue who unmasks her to be nothing but a scoundrel — albeit a dangerously handsome one. He may have rescued her from an attempted kidnapping, but she will not give in to his sensual seduction or to the wicked desire she begins to feel . . .

He is Edmund Hawkins, swashbuckling pirate turned reluctant gentleman, and he will not let the lovely Amy slip through his grasp, especially when he learns she's in greater peril than she could possibly know. He will do everything in his power to protect her — for this notorious scoundrel has truly, unbelievably, lost his heart . . .

"The sexy, dashing Hawkins brothers return, lifting readers' hearts and temperatures. Benedict employs intense emotions, a keen awareness of human nature and sensuality to enhance stories filled with action and adventure, unforgettable characters and unique plotlines."

Romantic Times Book Reviews,
Top Pick! review of *The Notorious Scoundrel*

How to Seduce a Pirate (book three)

The downtrodden daughter of a viscount, the Honorable Miss Holly Turner is desperate for money and assumes the secret identity of Lord H—the erotic artist—but her carefully crafted world turns on its ear when she stumbles into the room of one very handsome—and very naked—gentleman, mistaking him for her model.

Quincy Hawkins is chasing the dragon, hoping to outrun the demons from his past, but when an audacious—albeit beautiful—wench paints him in the buff, mayhem erupts. What is a gentleman pirate to do when scandal strikes? Marry the wench, of course. There's just one hitch. He won't bed her. Ever. His charming wife has already stolen from him his likeness, his freedom, and Quincy won't give her anything more . . . not even his body.

Holly can't believe her ears. A marriage in name alone? She will never have a wedding night? She will never know the pleasure of her husband's sensuous touch? Well, she won't stand for it. She intends to have a real marriage—with all the sensual benefits—even if it means seducing her stubborn pirate.

And don't miss *Too Great a Temptation* and *Too Dangerous to Desire* where The Hawkins Brothers first appeared as supporting characters—and stole readers' hearts!

Too Great a Temptation

A lord so sinful he is dubbed the "Duke of Rogues," Damian Westmore lives for pleasure—until the day his brother dies at the hands of pirates. Abandoning the libertine life to pursue revenge, Damian finds the criminals he seeks and joins their crew in disguise, waiting for the chance to strike the brigands down. But he never imagined there would be a woman on board—or that the stunning siren would inflame the very passions Damian swore to resist until his brother's death was avenged.

Beautiful, fiery Mirabelle Hawkins longs for the freedom of the high seas—so she stows away on her brother's pirate ship at the first opportunity. But she finds something more exciting than chase and plunder: a bold, handsome, secretive sailor whose touch makes her tremble with desire . . . but whose love is a cutlass that could destroy all she holds dear.

"Fans of historical romance will thoroughly enjoy this fresh take on the genre."

Publisher's Weekly,
Starred Review of *Too Great a Temptation*

Too Dangerous to Desire

Lonely and overcome with grief after a painful loss in his past, Adam Westmore walks the ocean's edge in solitude.

Forced to marry a depraved foreign prince, Evelyn Waye believes she has no choice but to throw herself from the jagged cliffs into the crashing surf below.

When Adam sees the enchanting woman in terrible danger, he rescues her from death and brings her back to his humble cottage. Hesitant to reveal his true identity as a distinguished lord, he nonetheless offers to protect her. And she needs protection, for the prince will find her — and harm her.

Evelyn wants to trust the handsome stranger who saved her life, but her cursed beauty has made her suspicious of all men . . . even one whose kindness disarms her, whose gentle touch inspires passion within her.

Soon Adam and Evelyn are consumed by desire . . . a dangerous desire that puts their very lives in peril.

"An outstanding read."

Romance Reader at Heart,
Top Pick! review of *Too Dangerous to Desire*

ABOUT THE AUTHOR

Alexandra Benedict is the author of several historical romances published by Avon Books. She also writes fiction as an Indie Author. Her work has received critical acclaim from *Booklist* and a starred review from *Publishers Weekly*. All of her books are translated into various languages. For more information visit: **www.AlexandraBenedict.ca**. Or friend her on FACEBOOK at **Alexandra Benedict Author**.

Made in the USA
Coppell, TX
07 July 2023

18838974R00118